# AFFAIR IN ARABY

*Talbot Mundy*

# Contents

CHAPTER I.................................................................................7

CHAPTER II...............................................................................12

CHAPTER III..............................................................................24

CHAPTER IV..............................................................................34

CHAPTER V ..............................................................................42

CHAPTER VI..............................................................................50

CHAPTER VII.............................................................................59

CHAPTER VIII............................................................................68

CHAPTER IX..............................................................................76

CHAPTER X................................................................................83

CHAPTER XI..............................................................................88

CHAPTER XII.............................................................................95

CHAPTER XIII...........................................................................104

CHAPTER XIV ..........................................................................116

CHAPTER XV............................................................................130

# AFFAIR IN ARABY

BY

Talbot Mundy

---

# CHAPTER I

"I'll make one to give this Feisul boy a hoist"

Whoever invented chess understood the world's works as some men know clocks and watches. He recognized a fact and based a game on it, with the result that his game endures. And what he clearly recognized was this: That no king matters much as long as your side is playing a winning game. You can leave your king in his corner then to amuse himself in dignified unimportance. But the minute you begin to lose, your king becomes a source of anxiety.

In what is called real life (which is only a great game, although a mighty good one) it makes no difference what you call your king. Call him Pope if you want to, or President, or Chairman. He grows in importance in proportion as the other side develops the attack. You've got to keep your symbol of authority protected or you lose.

Nevertheless, your game is not lost as long as your king can move. That's why the men who want to hurry up and start a new political era imprison kings and cut their heads off. With no head on his shoulders your king can only move in the direction of the cemetery, which is over the line and doesn't count.

I love a good fight, and have been told I ought to be ashamed of it. I've noticed, though, that the folk who propose to elevate my morals fight just as hard, and less cleanly, with their tongue than some of us do with our fists and sinews. I'm told, too, quite frequently that as an American I ought to be ashamed of fighting for a king. Dear old ladies of both sexes have assured me that it isn't moral to give aid and comfort to a gallant gentleman--a godless Mohammedan, too; which makes it much worse--who is striving gamely and without malice to keep his given word and save his country.

But if you've got all you want, do you know of any better fun than lending a hand while some man you happen to like gets his? I don't. Of course, some fellows want too much, and it's bad manners as well as waste of time to inflict your opinion on them. But given a reasonable purpose and a friend who needs your assistance, is there any better sport on earth than risking your own neck to help him put it over?

Walk wide of the man and particularly of the woman, who makes a noise about lining your pocket or improving your condition. An altruist is my friend James Schuyler Grim, but he makes less noise than a panther on a dark night; and I never knew a man less given to persuading you. He has one purpose, but almost never talks about it. It's a sure bet that if we hadn't struck up a close friendship, sounding each other out carefully as opportunity occurred, I would have been in the dark about it until this minute.

All the news of Asia from Alexandretta to the Persian Gulf and from Northern Turkestan to South Arabia reaches Grim's ears sooner or later. He earns his bread and butter knitting all that mess of cross-grained information into one intelligible pattern; after which he interprets it and acts suddenly without advance notices.

Time and again, lone-handed, he has done better than an army corps, by playing chief against chief in a land where the only law is individual interpretation of the Koran.

But it wasn't until our rescue of Jeremy Ross from near Abu Kem, that I ever heard Grim come out openly and admit that he was working to establish Feisul, third son of the King of Mecca, as king of just as many Arabs as might care to have him over them. That was the cat he had been keeping in a bag for seven years.

Right down to the minute when Grim, Jeremy and I sat down with Ben Saoud the Avenger on a stricken field at Abu Kem, and Grim and Jeremy played their hands so cleverly that the Avenger was made, unwitting guardian of Jeremy's secret gold-mine, and Feisul's open and sworn supporter in the bargain, the heart of Grim's purpose continued to be a mystery even to me; and I have been as intimate with him as any man.

He doles out what he has in mind as grudgingly as any Scot spends the shillings in his purse. But the Scots are generous when they have to be, and so is Grim.

There being nothing else for it on that occasion, he spilled the beans, the whole beans, and nothing but the beans. Having admitted us two to his secret, he dilated on it all the way back to Jerusalem, telling us all he knew of Feisul (which would fill a book), and growing almost lyrical at times as he related incidents in proof of his contention that Feisul, lineal descendant of the Prophet Mohammed, is the "whitest" Arab and most gallant leader of his race since Saladin.

Knowing Grim and how carefully suppressed his enthusiasm usually is, I couldn't help being fired by all he said on that occasion.

And as for Jeremy, well--it was like meat and drink to him. You meet men more or less like Jeremy Ross in any of earth's wild places, although you rarely meet his equal for audacity, irreverence and riotous good-fellowship. He isn't the only Australian by a long shot who upholds Australia by fist and boast and astounding gallantry, yet stays away from home. You couldn't fix Jeremy with concrete; he'd find some means of bursting any mould.

He had been too long lost in the heart of Arabia for anything except the thought of Sydney Bluffs and the homesteads that lie beyond to tempt him for the first few days.

"You fellers come with me," he insisted. "You chuck the Army, Grim, and I'll show you a country where the cows have to bend their backs to let the sun go down. Ha-ha! Show you women too--red-lipped girls in sunbonnets, that'll look good after the splay-footed crows you see out here. Tell you what: We'll pick up the Orient boat at Port Said--no P. and O. for me; I'm a passenger aboard ship, not a horrible example!-- and make a wake for the Bull's Kid. Murder! Won't the scoff taste good!

"We'll hit the Bull's Kid hard for about a week--mix it with the fellers in from way back--you know--dry-blowers, pearlers, spending it easy-- handing their money to Bessie behind the bar and restless because she makes it last too long; watch them a while and get in touch with all that's happening; then flit out of Sydney like bats out of--and hump blue--eh?"

"Something'll turn up; it always does. I've got money in the bank-- about, two thousand here in gold dust with me,--and if what you say's true, Grim, about me still being a trooper, then the Army owes me three years' back pay, and I'll have it or go to Buckingham Palace and tear off a piece of the King! We're capitalists, by

Jupiter!  Besides, you fellers agreed that if I shut down the mine at Abu Kem you'd join me and we'd be Grim, Ramsden and Ross."

"I'll keep the bargain if you hold me to it when the time comes," Grim answered.

"You bet I'll hold you to it!  Rammy here, and you and I could trade the chosen people off the map between us.  We're a combination.  What's time got to do with it?"

"We've got to use your mine," Grim answered.

"I'm game.  But let's see Australia first."

"Suppose we fix up your discharge, and you go home," Grim suggested.  "Come back when you've had a vacation, and by that time Ramsden and I will have done what's possible for Feisul.  He's in Damascus now, but the French have got him backed into a corner.  No money--not much ammunition--French propaganda undermining the allegiance of his men-- time working against him, and nothing to do but wait."

"What in hell have the French got to do with it?"

"They want Syria.  They've got the coast towns now.  They mean to have Damascus; and if they can catch Feisul and jail him to keep him out of mischief they will."

"But damn it!  Didn't they promise the Arabs that Feisul should be King of Syria, Palestine, Mesopotamia, and all that?"

"They did.  The Allies all promised, France included.  But since the Armistice the British have made a present of Palestine to the Jews, and the French have demanded Syria for themselves.  The British are pro-Feisul, but the French don't want him anywhere except dead or in jail. They know they've given him and the Arabs a raw deal;  and they seem to think the simplest way out is to blacken Feisul's character and ditch him.  If the French once catch him in Damascus he's done for and the Arab cause is lost."

"Why lost?" demanded Jeremy.  "There are plenty more Arabs."

"But only one Feisul.  He's the only man who can unite them all."

"I know a chance for him," said Jeremy.  "Let him come with us three to Australia.  There are thousands of fellers there who fought alongside him and don't care a damn for the French. They'll raise all the hell there is before they'll see him ditched."

"Uh-huh! London's the place for him," Grim answered. "The British like him, and they're ashamed of the way he's been treated. They'll give him Mesopotamia. Baghdad's the old Arab capital, and that'll do for a beginning; after that it's up to the Arabs themselves."

"Well? Where does my gold mine come in?" Jeremy asked.

"Feisul has no money. If it was made clear to him that he could serve the Arabs best by going to London, he'd consider it. The objection would be, though, that he'd have to make terms in advance with hog-financiers, who'd work through the Foreign Office to tie up all the oil and mine and irrigation concessions. If we tell him privately about your gold mine at Abu Kem he can laugh at financiers."

"All right," said Jeremy, "I'll give him the gold mine. Let him erect a modern plant and he'll have millions!"

"Uh-huh! Keep the mine secret. Let him go to London and arrange about Mespot. Just at present High Finance could find a hundred ways of disputing his title to the mine, but once he's king with the Arabs all rooting for him things'll be different. He'll treat you right when that time comes, don't worry."

"Worry? Me?" said Jeremy. "All that worries me is having to see this business through before we can make a wake for Sydney. I'm homesick. But never mind. All right, you fellers, I'll make one to give this Feisul boy a hoist!"

---

# CHAPTER II

"Atcha, Jimgrim sahib! Atcha!"

That conversation and Jeremy's conversion to the big idea took place on the way across the desert to Jerusalem--a journey that took us a week on camel-back--a rowdy, hot journey with the stifling simoom blowing grit into our followers' throats, who sang and argued alternately nevertheless. For, besides our old Ali Baba and his sixteen sons and grandsons, there were Jeremy's ten pickups from Arabia's byways, whom he couldn't leave behind because they knew the secret of his gold-mine.

Grim's authority is always at its height on the outbound trail, for then everybody knows that success, and even safety, depends on his swift thinking; on the way home afterward reaction sets in sometimes, because Arabs are made light-headed by success, and it isn't a simple matter to discipline free men when you have no obvious hold over them.

But that was where Jeremy came in. Jeremy could do tricks, and the Arabs were like children when he performed for them. They would be good if he would make one live chicken into two live ones by pulling it apart. They would pitch the tents without fighting if he would swallow a dozen eggs and produce them presently from under a camel's tail. If he would turn on his ventriloquism and make a camel say its prayers, they were willing to forgive--for the moment anyhow--even their nearest enemies.

So we became a sort of travelling sideshow, with Jeremy ballyhooing for himself in an amazing flow of colloquial Arabic, and hardly ever repeating the same trick.

All of which was very good for our crowd and convenient at the moment, but hardly so good for Jeremy's equilibrium. He is one of those handsome, perpetually youthful fellows, whose heads have been a wee mite turned by the sunshine of the world's warm smile. I don't mean by that that he isn't a tophole man, or a thorough-going friend with guts and gumption, who would chance his neck for anyone he likes without a second's hesitation, for he's every bit of that. He has horse sense, too, and isn't fooled by the sort of flattery that women lavish on men who have laughing eyes and a little dark moustache.

But he hasn't been yet in a predicament that he couldn't laugh or fight his way out of; he has never yet found a job that he cared to stick at for more than a year or two, and seldom one that could hold him for six months.

He jumps from one thing to another, finding all the world so interesting and amusing, and most folk so ready to make friends with him, that he always feels sure of landing softly somewhere over the horizon.

So by the time we reached Jerusalem friend Jeremy was ripe for almost any-thing except the plan we had agreed on. Having talked that over pretty steadily most of the way from Abu Kem, it seemed already about as stale and unattractive to him as some of his oldest tricks. And Jerusalem provided plenty of distraction. We hadn't been in Grim's quarters half an hour when Jeremy was up to his ears in a dispute that looked like separating us.

Grim, who wears his Arab clothes from preference and never gets into uniform if he can help it, went straight to the telephone to report briefly to headquarters. I took Jeremy upstairs to discard my Indian disguise and hunt out clothes for Jeremy that would fit him, but found none, I being nearly as heavy as Grim and Jeremy together. He had finished clowning in the kit I offered him, and had got back into his Arab things while I was shaving off the black whiskers with which Nature adorns my face whenever I neglect the razor for a few days, when an auto came tooting and roaring down the narrow street, and a moment later three staff officers took the stairs at a run. So far, good; that was unofficial, good-natured, human and entirely decent. The three of them burst through the bed room door, all grins, and took turns pumping with Jeremy's right arm--glad to see him--proud to know him--pleased to see him looking fit and well, and all that kind of thing. Even men who had fought all through the war had forgotten some of its red tape by that time, and Jeremy not being in uniform they treated him like a fellow human being. And he reciprocated, Australian fashion, free and easy, throwing up his long legs on my bed and yelling for somebody to bring drinks for the crowd, while they showered questions on him.

It wasn't until Jeremy turned the tables and began to question them that the first cloud showed itself.

"Say, old top," he demanded of a man who wore the crossed swords of a brigadier. "Grim tells me I'm a trooper. When can I get my discharge?"

The effect was instantaneous. You would have thought they had touched a leper by the way they drew themselves up and changed face.

"Never thought of that. Oh, I say--this is a complication. You mean...?"

"I mean this," Jeremy answered dryly, because nobody could have helped notice their change of attitude: "I was made prisoner by Arabs and carried off. That's more than three years ago. The war's over. Grim tells me all Australians have been sent home and discharged. What about me?"

"Um-m-m! Ah! This will have to be considered. Let's see; to whom did you surrender?"

"Damn you, I didn't surrender! I met Grim in the desert, and reported to him for duty."

"Met Major Grim, eh?"

"Yes," said Grim, appearing in the door. "I came across him in the desert; he reported for duty; I gave him an order, and he obeyed it. Everything's regular."

"Um-m-m! How'd you make that out--regular? Have you any proof he wasn't a deserter? He'll have to be charged with desertion and tried by court martial, I'm afraid. Possibly a mere formality, but it'll have to be done, you know, before he can be given a clear discharge. If he can't be proved guilty of desertion he'll be cleared."

"How long will that take?" Jeremy demanded.

His voice rang sharp with the challenge note that means debate has ceased and quarrel started. It isn't the right note for dissolving difficulties.

"Couldn't tell you," said the brigadier. "My advice to you is to keep yourself as inconspicuous as possible until the administrator gets back."

It was good advice, but Grim, standing behind the brigadier, made signals to Jeremy in vain. Few Australians talk peace when there is no peace, and when there's a fight in prospect they like to get it over.

"I remember you," said Jeremy, speaking rather, slowly, and throwing in a little catchy laugh that was like a war-cry heard through a microphone. "You were the Fusileer major they lent to the Jordan Highlanders--fine force that--no advance without security--lost two men, if I remember--snakebite one; the other shot for looting. Am I right? So they've made you a brigadier! Aren't you the staff officer they sent to strafe a regiment of Anzacs for going into action without orders? We chased you to cover! I can see you now running for fear we'd shoot you! Hah!"

Grim took the only course possible in the circumstances. The brigadier's neck was crimson, and Jeremy had to be saved somehow.

"Touch of sun, sir--that and hardship have unhinged him a bit. Suffers from delusions. Suppose I keep him here until the doctor sees him?"

"Um-m-m! Ah! Yes, you'd better. See he gets no whisky, will you? Too bad! Too bad! What a pity!"

Our three visitors left in a hurry, contriving to look devilish important. Grim followed them out.

"Rammy, old cock," said Jeremy, sprawling on the bed again and laughing, "don't look all that serious. Bring back your brigadier and I'll kiss him on both cheeks while you hold him! But say; suppose that doctor's one of these swabs who serve out number nine pills for shell-shock, broken leg, dyspepsia, housemaid's knee and the creeping itch? Suppose he swears I'm luny? What then?"

"Grim will find somebody to swear to anything once," I answered. "But you look altogether too dashed healthy--got to give the doctor-man a chance--here, get between the sheets and kid that something hurts you."

"Get out! The doc 'ud put a cast-iron splint on it, and order me into a hospital. How about toothache? That do? Do they give you bread and water for it?"

So toothache was selected as an alibi, and Jeremy wrapped his jaw in a towel, after jabbing his cheek with a pin so as to remember on which side the pain should be. But it was artifice wasted, for Grim had turned a better trick. He had found an Australian doctor in the hospital for Sikhs--the only other Australian in Jerusalem just then-- and brought him cooee-ing upstairs in a way that proved he knew the whole story already.

The autopsy, as he called it, was a riot. We didn't talk of anything but fights at Gaza--the surprise at Nazareth, when the German General Staff fled up the road on foot in its pyjamas--the three-day scrap at Nebi Samwil, when Australians and Turks took and retook the same hill half a dozen times, and parched enemies took turns drinking from one flask while the shells of both sides burst above them. It seems to have been almost like old-fashioned war in Palestine from their account of it, either side conceding that the other played the game.

When they had thrashed the whole campaign over from start to finish, making maps on my bed with hair brushes, razors and things, they got to talking of Australia; and that was all about fighting too: dog fights, fist fights between bullockies on the long road from Northern Queensland, riots in Perth when the pearlers came in off the Barrier Reef to spend their pay, rows in the big shearing sheds when the Union men objected to unskilled labour--you'd have thought Australia was one big battlefield, with nothing else but fights worth talking of from dawn till dark.

The doctor was one of those tightly-knit, dark-complexioned little men with large freckles and brown eyes, who surprise you with a mixture of intense domestic virtue and a capacity, that shouldn't mix with it at all, for turning up in all the un-expected places. You meet his sort everywhere, and they always have a wife along, who worships them and makes a home out of tin cans and packing-cases that would put the stay-at-home housekeepers to shame. They always have a picture on the wall of cows standing knee-deep in the water, and no matter what their circum-stances are, there's always something in reserve, for guests, offered frankly without apology. Never hesitate with those folk, but don't let them go too far, for they'll beggar themselves to help you in a tight place, if you'll let them. Ticknor his name was. He's a good man.

"Say, Grim, there's a case in the Sikh hospital that ought to interest you," he said at last. "Fellow from Damascus--Arab--one of Feisul's crowd. He wouldn't let them take him to the Zionist hospital--swore a Jew knifed him and that the others would finish the job if they got half a chance. They'd have been arguing yet, and he dead and buried, if I hadn't gone shopping with Mabel. She saw the crowd first (I was in Noureddin's store) and jabbed her way in with her umbrella--she yelled to me and I bucked the line.

"The Jews wanted to tell me I had no right to take that chap to the Sikh hospi-tal, and no more had I; so I plugged him up a bit, and put him in a cab, and let him take himself there, Mabel and me beside him. Seeing I was paying for the cab, I didn't see why Mabel should walk. Of course, once we had him in there he was too sick to be moved;  but the Army won't pay for him, so I sent a bill to the Zionists, and they returned it with a rude remark on the margin.  Maybe I can get the money out of Feisul some day; otherwise I'm stuck."

"I'll settle that," said Grim. "What's the tune he plays?"

"Utter mystery.  Swears a Jew stabbed him, but that Damascus outfit blame the Jews for everything.  He's only just down from Damascus.  I think he's one of Feisul's officers, although he's not in uniform-- prob'ly on a secret mission.  Suppose you go and see him?  But say, watch out for the doc on duty--he's a meddler. Tell him nothing!"

"Sure.  How about Jeremy?  What's the verdict?"

"What do you want done with him?"

"I want him out of reach of trouble here pending his discharge. No need to certify him mad, is there?"

"Mad?  All Australians are mad.  None of us need a certificate for that. Have you arrested him?"

"Not yet."

"Then you're too late!  He's suffering from bad food and exposure.  The air of Jerusalem's bad for him, and he's liable to get pugnacious if argued with.  That runs in the blood.  I order him off duty, and shall recommend him within twenty minutes to the P.M.O. for leave of absence at his own expense. If you know of any general who dares override the P.M.O. I'll show you a brass hat in the wind.  Come on; d'you want to bet on it?"

"Will the P.M.O. fall?" asked Grim.

"Like a new chum off a brumby.  Signs anything I shove under his nose. Comes round to our house to eat Mabel's damper and syrup three nights a week.  You bet he'll sign it:  Besides, he's white;  pulled out of the firing-line by an Australian at Gaza, and hasn't forgotten it.  He'd sign anything but checks to help an Anzac.  I'll be going.

"You trot up to the slaughter-shop, Grim, and interview that Arab--Sidi bin Something-or-Other--forget his name--he lies in number nineteen cot on the left-hand side of the long ward, next to a Pathan who's shy both legs.  You can't mistake him. I'll write out a medical certificate for Jeremy and follow. And say; wait a minute! What price the lot of you eating Mabel's chow tonight at our house? We don't keep a cook, so you won't get poisoned. That's settled; I'll tell Mabel you're coming. Tootleloo!"

But there was a chance that the brigadier might carry resentment to the point of sending up a provost-marshal's guard to arrest Jeremy on the well-known principle that a bird in the hand can be strafed more easily than one with a medical certificate. The bush was the place for our bird until such time as the P.M.O.'s signature should adorn the necessary piece of paper; so we three rode up in a cab together to the Sikh hospital, and had a rare time trying to get in.

You see, there was a Sikh on guard outside, who respected nothing under heaven but his orders. He wouldn't have known Grim in any event, being only recently from India; Grim's uniform would have passed him in, but he and Jeremy were still arrayed as Arabs, and my civilian clothes entitled me in the sentry's opinion to protection lest I commit the heinous sin of impertinence. An Arab in his eyes was as an insect, and a white man, who consorted with such creatures, not a person to be taken seriously.

But our friend Narayan Singh was in the hospital, enjoying the wise veteran's prerogative of resting on full pay after his strenuous adventures along with us at Abu Kem. There was nothing whatever the matter with him. He recognized Grim's voice and emerged through the front door with a milk-white smile flashing in the midst of newly-curled black hair--dignified, immense, and full of instant understanding.

Grim said a few words to Narayan Singh in Arabic, which so far as the sentry was concerned wasn't a language, but Narayan Singh spoke in turn in Punjabi, and the man just out from India began to droop like Jonah's gourd under the old soldier's scorn.

In consequence we got a full salute with arms presented, and walked in without having to trouble anybody in authority, Narayan Singh leading with the air of an old-time butler showing royalty to their rooms. He even ascertained in an aside, that the doctor of the day was busy operating, and broke that good news with consummate tact:

"The sahibs' lightest wish is law, but if they should wish to speak with the doctor sahib, it would be necessary to call him forth from the surgery, where he works behind locked doors. Is it desired that I should summon him?"

"Operation serious?" asked Grim, and neither man smiled. It was perfect acting.

"Very, sahib. He removes the half of a sepoy's liver."

"Uh! Couldn't think of interrupting him. Too bad! Lead the way."

But we didn't enter the ward until Narayan Singh and an orderly had placed two screens around number nineteen cot, in the way they do when a man is dying, and had placed three chairs at the bedside contrary to the regulations printed on the wall. Then Narayan Singh stood on guard outside the screens, but didn't miss much of the conversation, I believe.

The man in bed was wounded badly, but not fatally, and though his eyes blazed with fever he seemed to have some of his wits about him. He recognized Grim after staring hard at him for about a minute.

"Jimgrim!"

"Sidi bin Tagim, isn't it? Well, well I thought it might be you," said Grim, speaking the northern dialect of Arabic, which differs quite a bit from that spoken around Jerusalem.

"Who are these?" asked the man in bed, speaking hoarsely as he stared first at Jeremy and then at me.

"Jmil Ras, a friend of mine," Grim answered.

"And that one?"

He didn't like the look of me at all. Western clothes and a shaven face spell nothing reassuring to the Arab when in trouble; he has been "helped" by the foreigner a time or two too often.

"An American named Ramsden. Also a friend of mine."

"Oh! An Amirikani? A hakim?"

"No. Not a doctor. Not a man to fear. He is a friend of Feisul."

"On whose word?"

"Mine," Grim answered.

Sidi bin Tagim nodded. He seemed willing to take Grim's word for anything.

"Why did you say a Jew stabbed you?" Grim asked suddenly.

"So that they might hang a Jew or two. Wallah! Are the Jews not at the bottom of all trouble? If a Greek should kill a Maltese it would be a Jew who planned it! May the curse of Allah change their faces and the fire of Eblis consume them!"

"Did you see the man who stabbed you?"

"Yes."

And was he a Jew?"

"Jimgrim, you know better than to ask that! A Jew always hires another to do the killing. He who struck me was a hireling, who shall die by my hand, as Allah is my witness. But may Allah do more to me and bring me down into the dust un-buried unless I make ten Jews pay for this!"

"Any one Jew in particular?" Grim asked, and the man in bed closed up like a clam that has been touched.

He was a strange-looking fellow--rather like one of those lean Spaniards whom Goya used to paint, with a scant beard turning grey, and hollow cheeks. He had thrown off the grey army blanket because fever burned him, and his lean, hard muscles stood out as if cast in bronze.

"But for the Jews, Feisul would be king of all this land this minute!" he said suddenly, and closed up tight again.

Grim smiled. He nearly always does smile when apparently at a loose end. At moments when most cross-examiners would browbeat he grows sympathetic--humours his man, and, by following whatever detour offers, gets back on the trail again.

"How about the French?" he asked.

"May Allah smite them! They are all in the pay of Jews!"

"Can you prove it?"

"Wallah! That I can!"

Grim looked incredulous. Those baffling eyes of his twinkled with quiet amuse-ment, and the man in bed resented it.

"You laugh, Jimgrim, but if you would listen I might tell you something."

But Grim only smiled more broadly than ever.

"Sidi bin Tagim, you're one of those fanatics who think the world is all leagued against you. Why should the Jews think you sufficiently important to be mur-dered?"

"Wallah! There are few who hold the reins of happenings as I do."

"If they'd killed you they'd have stopped the clock, eh?"

"That is as Allah may determine. I am not dead."

"Have you friends in Jerusalem?"

"Surely."

"Strange that they haven't been to see you."

"Wallah! Not strange at all."

"I see. They regard you as a man without authority, who might make trouble and leave other men to face it, eh?"

"Who says I have no authority?"

"Well, if you could prove you have--"

"What then?" the man in bed demanded, trying to sit up. "Feisul, for instance, is a friend of mine, and these men with me are his friends too. You have no letter, of course, for that would be dangerous..."

"Jimgrim, in the name of the Most High, I swear I had a letter! He who stabbed me took it. I--"

"Was the letter from Feisul?"

"Malaish--no matter. It was sealed, and bore a number for the signature. If you can get that letter for me, Jimgrim--but what is the use! You are a servant of the British."

"Tell me who stabbed you and I'll get you the letter."

"No, for you are clever. You would learn too much. Better tell the doctor of this place to hurry up and heal me; then I will attend to my own affairs."

"I'd like to keep you out of jail, if that's possible," Grim answered. "You and I are old acquaintances, Sidi bin Tagim. But of course, if you're here to sow sedition, and should there be a document at large in proof of it, which document should fall into the hands of the police-- well, I couldn't do much for you then. You'd better tell me who stabbed you, and I'll get after him."

"Ah! But if you get the letter?"

"I shall read it, of course."

"But to whom will you show it?"

"Perhaps to my friends here."

"Are they bound by your honour?"

"I shall hold them so."

There was the glint in Grim's eye now that should warn anyone who knew him that the scent was hot; added to the fact that the rest of his expression suggested waning interest, that look of his forebode fine hunting.

"There's one other I might consult," he admitted casually. "On my way here I saw one of Feisul's staff captains driving in a cab toward the Jaffa Gate."

The instant effect of that remark was to throw the wounded man into a paroxysm of mingled rage and fear. He almost threw a fit. His already bloodless face grew ashy grey and livid blue alternately, and he would have screamed at Grim if the cough that began to rack his whole body would have let him. As it was, he gasped out unintelligible words and sought to make Grim understand by signs. And Grim apparently did understand.

"Very well," he laughed, "tell me who stabbed you and I won't mention your name to Staff-Captain Abd el Kadir."

"And these men? Will they say nothing?"

"Not a word. Who stabbed you?"

"Yussuf Dakmar! May Allah cut him off from love and mercy!"

"Golly!" exploded Jeremy, forgetting not to talk English. "There's a swine for you! Yussuf Dakmar's the son of a sea-cook who used to sell sheep to the Army four times over--drive 'em into camp and get a receipt--drive 'em out again next night-- bring 'em back in the morning-- get a receipt again--drive 'em off--bring 'em back- -us chaps too busy shifting brother Turk to cotton on. He'll be the boy I kicked out of camp once. Maybe remembers it too. I'll bet his backbone's twanging yet! Lead me to him, Grim, old cock, I'd like another piece of him!"

But Grim was humming to himself, playing piano on the bed-sheet with his fingers.

"Is that man not an Arab?" asked the fellow in bed, taking alarm all over again.

"Arab your aunt!" laughed Jeremy: "I eat Arabs! I'm the only original genuine woolly bad man from way back! I'm the plumber who pulled the plug out of Arabia! You know English? Good! You know what a dose of salts is then? You've seen it work? Experienced it, maybe? Hah! You'll understand me. I'm a grain of the Epsom Salt that went through Beersheba, time the Turks had all the booze in sight and we were thirsty. Muddy booze it was too--oozy booze--not fit for washing hogs! Ever heard of Anzacs? Well, I'm one of 'em. Now you know what the scorpion who stung you's up against! You lie there and think about it, cocky; I'll show you his shirt tomorrow morning."

"Suppose we go now," suggested Grim. "I've got the drift of this thing. Get the rest elsewhere."

"You can fan that Joskins for a lot more yet," Jeremy objected. "The plug's pulled. He'll flow if you let him."

Grim nodded.

"Sure he would. Don't want too much from him. Don't want to have to arrest him. Get me?"

"Come on then," answered Jeremy, "I've promised him a shirt!"

Beyond the screen Narayan Singh stood like a statue, deaf, dumb, immovable. Even his eyes were fixed with a blank stare on the wall opposite.

"How much did you hear?" Grim asked him.

"I, sahib? I am a sick man. I have been asleep."

"Dream anything?"

"As your honour pleases!"

"Hospital's stuffy, isn't it? Think you could recover health more rapidly out-doors? Sick-leave continued of course, but--how about a little exercise?"

The Sikh's eyes twinkled.

"Sahib, you know I need exercise!"

"I'll speak to the doctor for you. In case he signs a new certificate, report to me tonight."

"Atcha, Jimgrim sahib! Atcha!"

# CHAPTER III

"Hum Dekta hai"

Like most of the quarters occupied by British officers, the house occupied by Major Roger Ticknor and his wife Mabel was "enemy property," and its only virtue consisted in its being rent free. Grim, Jeremy, little Ticknor and his smaller wife, and I sat facing across a small deal table with a stuttering oil-lamp between us. In a house not far away some Orthodox Jews, arrayed in purple and green and orange, with fox-fur around the edges of their hats, were drunk and celebrating noisily the Feast of Esther; so you can work out the exact date if you're curious enough. The time was nine p.m. We had talked the Anzac hurricane-drive through Palestine all over again from the beginning, taking world-known names in vain and doing honour to others that will stay unsung for lack of recognition, when one of those unaccountable pauses came, and for the sake of breaking silence, Mabel Ticknor asked a question. She was a little, plucky, pale-faced thing whom you called instinctively by her first name at the end of half an hour--a sort of little mother of loose-ended men, who can make silk purses out of sows' ears, and wouldn't know how to brag if she were tempted.

"Say, Jim," she asked, turning her head quickly like a bird toward Grim on my left, "what's your verdict about that man from Syria that Roger took in a cab to the Sikh hospital? I'm out a new pair of riding breeches if Roger has to pay the bill for him. I want my money's worth. Tell me his story."

"Go ahead and buy the breeches, Mabel. I'll settle that bill," he answered.

"No, you won't, Jim! You're always squandering money. Half your pay goes to the scallywags you've landed in jail. This one's up to Roger and me; we found him."

Grim laughed.

"I can charge his keep under the head of 'information paid for.' I shall sign the voucher without a qualm."

"You'd get blood out of a stone, Jim! Go on, tell us!"

"I'm hired to keep secrets as well as discover them," Grim answered, smiling broadly.

"Of course you are," she retorted. "But I know all Roger's secrets, and he's a doctor, mind you! Am I right, Roger? Come along! There are no servants--no eavesdroppers. Wait. I'll put tea on the table, and then we'll all listen."

She made tea Australian fashion in a billy, which is quick and simple, but causes alleged dyspepsia cures to sell well all the way from Adelaide to the Gulf of Carpentraia.

"You'll have to tell her, Jim," said Jeremy.

"Mabel's safe as an iron roof," put in her husband. "Noisy in the rain, but doesn't leak."

But neither man nor woman could have extracted a story from James Schuyler Grim unless it suited him to tell it. Mabel Ticknor is one of those honest little women who carry men's secrets with them up and down the world. Being confided in by nearly every man who met her was a habit. But Grim tells only when the telling may accomplish something, and I wondered, as he laid his elbow on the table to begin, just what use he meant to make of Mabel Ticknor. He uses what he knows as other level-headed men use coin, spending thriftily for fair advantage.

"That is secret," he began, as soon as Mabel had dumped the contents of the billy into a huge brown teapot. "I expect Narayan Singh here presently. He'll have a letter with him, taken from the Syrian who stabbed that man in the hospital."

"Whoa, hoss!" Jeremy interrupted. "You mean you've sent that Sikh to get the shirt of Yussuf Dakmar?"

Grim nodded.

"That was my job," Jeremy objected.

"Whoa, hoss, yourself, Jeremy!" Grim answered. "You'd have gone down into the bazaar like a bull into a china-shop. Narayan Singh knows where to find him. If he shows fight, he'll be simply handed over to the Sikh patrol for attacking a man in uniform, and by the time he reaches the lock-up that letter will be here on the table between us."

"All the same, that's a lark you've done me out of," Jeremy insisted. "That Yussuf Dakmar's a stinker. I know all about him. Two whole squadrons had to eat lousy biscuit for a week because that swab sold the same meat five times over. But I'll get him yet!"

"Well, as I was saying," Grim resumed, "there's a letter in Jerusalem that's supposed to be from Feisul. But when Feisul writes anything he signs his name to it, whereas a number is the signature on this. Now that fellow Sidi bin Tagim in the hospital is an honest old kite in his way. He's a great rooter for Feisul. And the only easy way to ditch a man like Feisul, who's as honest as the day is long, and no man's fool, is to convince his fanatical admirers that for his own sake he ought to be forced along a certain course. The game's as old as Adam. You fill up a man like Sidi bin Tagim with tales about Jews--convince him that Jews stand between Feisul and a kingdom--and he'll lend a hand in any scheme ostensibly directed against Jews. Get me?"

"So would I!" swore Jeremy. "I'm against 'em too! I camped alongside the Jordan Highlanders one time when--"

But we had had that story twice that evening with variations. He was balancing his chair on two legs, so I pushed him over backward, and before he could pick himself up again Grim resumed.

"Feisul is in Damascus, and the Syrian Convention has proclaimed him king. That don't suit the French, who detest him. The feeling's mutual. When Feisul went to Paris for the Peace Conference, the French imagined he was easy. They thought, here's another of these Eastern princes who can be taken in the old trap. So they staged a special performance at the Opera for him, and invited him to supper afterward behind the scenes with the usual sort of ladies in full war-paint in attendance."

"Shall we cut that too?" suggested Mabel.

"Sure. Feisul did! He's not that kind of moth. Ever since then the French have declared he's a hypocrite; and because he won't yield his rights they've been busy inventing wrongs of their own and insisting on immediate adjustment. The French haven't left one stone unturned that could irritate Feisul into making a false move."

"To hell with them!" suggested Jeremy, reaching for more tea.

"But Feisul's not easy to irritate," Grim went on. "He's one of those rare men, who get born once in an epoch, who force you to believe that virtue isn't extinct. He's almost like a child in some things--like a good woman in others--and a man of iron courage all the time, who can fire Arabs in the same way Saladin did five centuries ago."

"He looks like a saint," said Jeremy. "I've seen him."

"But he's no soft liver," continued Grim. "He was brought up in the desert among Bedouins, and has their stoical endurance with a sort of religious patience added. Gets that maybe from being a descendant of the Prophet."

"Awful sort to have to fight, that kind are," said Jeremy. "They wear you down!"

"So the French decided some time ago to persuade Feisul's intimates to make a bad break which he couldn't repudiate."

"Why don't he cut loose with forty or fifty thousand men and boot the French into the sea?" demanded Jeremy. "I'll make one to help him! I knew a Frenchman once, who--"

"We'll come to that presently," said Grim. "I dare say you didn't hear of Verdun."

"Objection sustained. Hand it to 'em. They've got guts," grinned Jeremy. "Fire away, old top."

"Well, they ran foul of an awkward predicament, which is that there are some darned decent fellows among the officers of their army of occupation. There's more than a scattering of decent gentlemen who don't like dirt. I won't say they tell Feisul secrets, or disobey orders; but if you want to give a man   a square deal there are ways of doing it without sending him telegrams."

Mabel put the tea back on the kerosene stove to stew, with an extra handful of black leaves in it. Grim continued:

"Another thing: The French are half afraid that if they take the field against Feisul on some trumped-up pretext, he'll get assistance from the British. They could send him things he needs more than money, and can't get. Ninety-nine per cent of the British are pro-Feisul. Some of them would risk their jobs to help him in a pinch. The French have got to stall those men before they can attack Feisul safely."

"How d'you mean--stall 'em?" demanded Jeremy. "Not all the British are fools--only their statesmen, and generals, and sixty percent of the junior officers and rank and file. The rest don't have to be fed pap from a bottle; they're good men. Takes more than talk to stall that kind off a man they like."

"You've got the idea, Jeremy. You have to show them. Well, why not stir up revolution here in Palestine in Feisul's name? Why not get the malcontents to murder Jews wholesale, with propaganda blowing full blast to make it look as if Feisul's hand is directing it all? It's as simple as falling off a log. French agents who look like honest Arabs approach the most hairbrained zealots who happen to be on the inside with Feisul, and suggest to them that the French and British are allies; therefore the only way to keep the British from helping the French will be to start red-hot trouble in Palestine that will keep the British busy protecting themselves and the Jews.

"The secret agents point out that although Feisul is against anything of the sort, he must be committed to it for his own sake. And they make great capital out of Feisul's promise that he will protect the Jews if recognized as king of independent Syria. Kill all the Jews beforehand, so there won't be any for him to protect when the time comes--that's the argument."

Mabel interrupted.

"Haven't you warned Feisul?"

She had both elbows on the table and her chin between her hands, and I dare say she had listened in just that attitude to fifty inside stories that the newspapers would scatter gold in vain to get.

"I sure did. And he has sent one of his staff down here to keep an eye on things. I saw him this afternoon riding in a cab toward the Jaffa Gate. I said as much to that fellow in the hospital, and he was scared stiff at the idea of my recovering the supposed Feisul letter and showing it to an officer who is really in Feisul's confidence. That--I mean the man's fear--linked everything up."

"You talk like Sherlock Holmes," laughed Jeremy. "I'll bet you a new hat nothing comes of it."

"That bet's on," Grim answered. "It's to be a female hat, and Mabel gets it. Order an expensive one from Paris, Mabel; Jeremy shall pay. We've lots of other information. The troops here have been warned of an intended massacre of Jews. The arrival of this letter probably puts a date to it.

"But it puts a date to something else on which the whole future of the Near East hangs; and that means the future of half the world, and maybe the whole of it, because about three hundred million Mohammedans are watching Feisul and will govern themselves accordingly. India, Persia, Mesopotamia, Egypt, all Northern Africa--there's almost no limit to what depends on Feisul's safety; and the French can't or won't understand that."

There came the sound of heavy ammunition boots outside on the stone step, followed by a cough that I believe I could recognize among a thousand. Narayan Singh coughs either of two ways--once, deep bass, for all's well; twice, almost falsetto, for a hint of danger. This time it was the single deep bass cough. But it was followed after half a minute by the two high-pitched barks, and Grim held up a hand for silence. At the end of perhaps a minute there came from the veranda a perfect imitation of the lascar's ungrammatical, whining singsong from a fo'castle-head:

"Hum dekta hai!--I'm on the watch."

Grim nodded--to himself, I suppose, for none had spoken to him.

"Do you mind stepping out and getting that letter from him, Ramsden? Keep in the shadow, please, and give him this pistol; he may need it."

So I slipped out through the screen door and spent a minute looking for Narayan Singh. I'm an old hunter, but it wasn't until Narayan Singh deliberately moved a hand to call attention to himself that I discovered him within ten feet of me.

The risk of being seen from the street in case some spy were lurking out there was obvious. So I walked all the way round the house, and came and stood below him on his left hand where the house cast impenetrable shadow; but though I took my time and moved stealthily he heard me and passed me a letter through the veranda rails, accepting the pistol in exchange without comment.

I could see him distinctly from that angle. His uniform on one side was torn almost into rags, and his turban was all awry, as if he had lost it in a scuffle and hadn't spared time to rewind it properly--a sure sign of desperate haste; for a male tiger in the spring-time is no more careful of his whiskers than a Sikh is of the thirty yards of cloth he winds around his head.

As he didn't speak or make any more movement than was necessary to pass me the letter and take the pistol, I returned the way I had come, entered by the back door, tossed the letter to Grim, and crept back again to bear a hand in case of need. Grim said nothing, but Jeremy followed me, and two minutes later the Australian and I were crouching in darkness below the veranda. This time I don't think Narayan Singh was aware of friends at hand.

His eyes were fixed on the slightly lighter gap in a dark wall that was the garden gate but looked more like a dim hole leading into a cave. There being no other entrance that we knew of, Jeremy and I doubled up on the same job, and a rat couldn't have come through without one of the three of us detecting him. If we had had our senses with us we might have realized that Narayan Singh was perfectly capable of watching that single narrow space, and have used our own eyes to better advantage. However, we're all three alive today, and two of us learned a lesson.

It wasn't long--perhaps five minutes--before a man showed himself outside the gate, like a spectre dodging this and that way in response to unearthly impulse. Once or twice he started forward, as if on the point of sneaking in, but thought better of it and retreated. Once his attitude suggested that he might be taking aim with a pistol; but if that was so, he chose not to waste a shot or start an alarm by firing at a mark he couldn't see. What he did accomplish was to keep six keen eyes fixed on him.

And that gave three other men their chance to gain an entrance at the rear of the wall in the garden, and creep up unawares. It was probably sheer accident that led all three of them along the far side of the house, but it was fortunate for Jeremy and me, for otherwise cold steel between our shoulder-blades would likely have been our first intimation of their presence.

We never suspected their existence until they gained the veranda by the end opposite to where we waited; and I think they would have done their murder if the man outside the gate hadn't lost his head from excitement, or some similar emotion and tried to make a signal to them. All three had brought up against the end window, where a shade torn in two places provided a good view into the room in which Grim, Mabel and the doctor were still sitting. Each of them had a pistol, and their intention didn't admit of doubt.

"Are you there, sahib?" Narayan Singh whispered.

But Jeremy and I were aware of them almost as soon as he, and rather than make a noise by vaulting the veranda rail, we took the longer route by way of the front steps. Jeremy, who was wearing sandals, kicked them off and not having to creep so carefully, moved faster.

Of course, the obvious question is, why didn't Narayan Singh shoot? I had a pistol too; why didn't I use it? Well, I'll tell you. None but the irresponsible criminal shoots a man except in obedience to orders or in self-defence.

You may argue that those three night-prowlers might have shot Ticknor and his wife and Grim through the window while we aired our superior virtue. The answer to that is, that they didn't, although that was their intention. Narayan Singh, already once that night in danger of his life, and a "godless, heathen Sikh," as I have heard a missionary call him, pocketed the pistol I had given him before proceeding to engage, he being also a white man by the proper way of estimating such things.

Jeremy was first on the scene of action, with Narayan Singh close behind him, and I was quite a bit behind, for I tripped against the top step in my hurry. The noise I made gave the alarm, and the three Arabs twisted round like cornered scorpions. I guess they couldn't see us well at first, having been staring through the torn shade into the lighted room.

Their pistols were cocked, but Jeremy's fist landed in the nearest man's face before he could shoot, and he went crashing backwards into his friend behind, whose head disappeared for a moment through the window-pane, and the only blood shed on that occasion came from the first man's nose and the back of the second man's neck where the smashed glass slit a gash in it.

The third man fired wildly at me, and missed, a fraction of a second before Narayan Singh landed on him with hands and feet; whereat the man in the street emptied his pistol at me and ran away. I was in two minds whether to give chase to him, but made the wrong decision, being heavy on my feet and none too fond of running, so the big fish got away.

But even with my help added, the three less important fish still gave a lot of trouble, for they fought like wild cats, using teeth and finger- nails; and the doctor and his wife and Grim were all out lending a hand before we had them finally convinced that the game was up. Mabel trussed up the worst man with a clothes line, while I sat on him.

I expected to see a crowd around the house by that time, but Jerusalem works otherwise than some cities. The sound of a pistol-shot sends everybody hurrying for cover, lest some enemy accuse them afterwards of having had a hand in the disturbance. And the nearest police post was a mile away. So we had our little outrage all to ourselves, although strange tales went the rounds of the Holy City that night, and two weeks later several European newspapers printed a beautiful account of a midnight massacre of Jews.

We dragged our prisoners into the sitting-room, and stood them up in front of Grim after the doctor and Mabel had attended to their hurts, which weren't especially serious; although nobody need expect to get in the way of Jeremy's fist and feel comfortable for several hours afterwards. The cut made in the second man's neck by broken glass needed several stitches, but the third man was only winded from having been sat on, and of course he was much more sorry for himself than either of the other two--a fact that Grim noted.

There was another noticeable circumstance that shed light on human nature and Grim's knowledge of it. They were all three eager to tell their story, although not necessarily the same story; whereas Narayan Singh, who knew that every word he might say would be believed implicitly, was in no hurry to tell his at all.

Now when you're dealing with Eastern and near-Eastern people of the sort who lie instinctively (and it may be that this applies to the West as well) it's a good plan to establish, if you can, a basis of truth for them to build their tale on; because the truth acts like acid on untruth. They're going to lie in any case; but lies told without any reference to truth knit better than when invented at a moment's notice to explain away another's straightforward statement. There's a plausible theory that culprits taken in the act are best examined in secret, one by one, in ignorance of all the evidence against them.

The wise method is to let them hear the evidence against themselves. Nine times out of ten they will accept that as unanswerable, and strive to twist its meaning or smother it under a mass of lies. But the truth they have accepted, as I have said, works just like acid and destroys their argument almost as fast as they build it up. In the few cases when that doesn't happen, they break down altogether and confess.

Anyhow, Grim, who taught me what I have just written, refused to listen to their bleating until Narayan Singh first told in their hearing all that he knew about the night's events. They were forced to sit down on the floor and listen to him like three coffee-shop loungers being told a story; and I don't doubt that the effect was strengthened by the Sikh's standing facing them, for the contrast was as between jackals and a lion.

Not that they were small men, for they weren't, or mere ten-dollar assassins picked up in the suk. They looked well fed, and wore fine linen, whereas Narayan Singh was in rags and had lost weight in our recent desert marching, so that his cheek-bones stood out and he looked superficially much more like a man at bay than they did.

But their well-cared-for faces were lean in the wrong place, and puffy under the eyes. In place of courage they flaunted an insolent leer, and the smile intended to convey self-confidence betrayed to a close observer anxiety bordering on panic.

The most offensive part about them really was their feet, which are indices of character too often overlooked. They had come to their task in slippers, which they had kicked off before reaching the veranda, and instead of the firm, tough feet that a real man stands on, what they displayed as they squatted were subtle, soft things, not exactly flabby, but even more suggestive of treachery than their thin beaks and shifty eyes.

To sum them up, they were dandies, of the kind who join the Young Turk Party and believe the New Era can be distilled of talk and tricks; and they looked like mean animals compared to that staunch conservative Narayan Singh, who, nevertheless, is not without his own degree of subtlety.

## CHAPTER IV

"I call this awful!"

Sahib, in accordance with instructions I proceeded to Christian Street to the place you spoke of, where I found Yussuf Dakmar drinking coffee and smoking in company with these men and others. They did not see me in the beginning, because I entered by the door of a house threescore and five paces farther down the street; and having by that means gained the roof I descended to a gallery built of stone above one end of the coffee-shop, and there lay concealed among evil-smelling bags.

"They conversed in Arabic; and presently when other men had entered, some of whose names I overheard and wrote down on this slip of paper, Yussuf Dakmar locked the outer door, turning the great key twice and setting a chain in place as well. Then he stood on a red stool having four short legs, with his back to the door that he had locked, and spoke in the manner of one who stirs a multitude, gesticulating greatly.

"The argument he made was thus: He said that Jerusalem is a holy city, and Palestine a holy land; and that promises are all the more sacred if given in connection with religious matters; whereat they all applauded greatly. Nevertheless, a little later on he mocked at all religion, and they applauded that too. He said that the Allies, persuaded thereto by the British, had made a promise to the Emir Feisul on the strength of which the Arabs made common war with the Allies against the Turks and Germans, losing of their own a hundred thousand men and untold money.

"So, sahib. Next he asked them how much of that promise made by the Allies to Emir Feisul as the leader of the Arabs had been kept, or was likely to be kept; and they answered in one voice, 'None of it!' Whereat he nodded, as a teacher nods gravely when the pupils have their lesson well by heart, and said presently in a voice like that of a Guru denouncing sin: 'A woman's promise is a little matter; who believes it? When it is broken all men laugh. A promise extorted under threat or torture is not binding, since he who made the promise was not free to govern his own conduct; that is law. A promise made in business,' said he, 'is a contract contingent on circumstances and subject to litigation. But a promise made in wartime by a nation is a pledge set down in letters of blood. Whoever breaks it is guilty of blood; and whoever fails to smite dead the breaker of that oath, commits treason against Allah!'

"They applauded that speech greatly, sahib, and when they grew silent he bade them look about and judge for themselves at whose door the breaking of that sacred promise really lay. 'Show me,' said he, 'one trace of Arab government in all Palestine. Who owns the land?' he asked them. 'Arabs!' said they. 'Yet to whom has the country been given?' he shouted. 'To the Jews!' they answered; and he grew silent for a while, like a teacher whose class has only given half the answer to a question until presently one man growled out, 'To the sword with the Jews in the name of Allah!' and the others echoed that which satisfied him, for he smiled, nevertheless not using those words himself. And presently he continued:

"'We in this room are men of enlightenment. We are satisfied to leave past and future to speculations of idle dreamers. For us the present. So we attach no value to the fact that Feisul is descended in a straight line from the founder of the Moslem faith; for that is a superstition as foolish in its way as Christianity or any other creed. But who is there like Feisul who can unite all Arabs under one banner?'

"They answered, sahib, that Feisul is the only living man who can accomplish that, making many assertions in his praise, Yussuf Dakmar nodding approval as each spoke. 'Yet,' said he when they had finished, 'Feisul is also fallible. In certain ways he is a fool, and principally in this: That he insists on keeping his own promises to men who have broken their own promises to him.' And like pupils in a class who recite their lesson, they all murmured that such a course as that is madness.

"'So,' said he, 'we are clear on that point. We are not altruists, nor religious fanatics, nor slaves, but men of common sense who have a business in view. We are not Feisul's servants, but he ours. We make use of him, not he of us. If he persists in a wrong course, we must force him into the right one, for the day of autocratic government is past and the hour has come when those who truly represent the people have the first right to direct all policy. If the right is still withheld from them, they must take it. And it is we in this room who truly represent the Arab cause, on whom lies the responsibility of forcing Feisul's hand!'

"Well, sahib, these three prisoners who sit here offered, at once to go to Damascus and kill the men who are advising Feisul wrongly. They said that if they were given money they could easily hire Damascenes to do the dagger work, there being, as the sahib doubtless knows, a common saying in these parts about Damascus folk and sharp steel. Whereat Yussuf Dakmar suddenly assumed a sneering tone of voice, saying that he preferred men for his part with spunk enough to do such work themselves, and there was an argument, they protesting and he mocking them, until at last this man, whose neck the glass cut, demanded of him whether he, Yussuf Dakmar, was not in truth an empty boaster who would flinch at bloodshed.

"He seemed to have been waiting for just that, sahib, for he smirked and threw a chest. 'I am a man,' said he, 'of example as well as precept. I have done what I saw fit to do! I make no boasts,' said he, 'for a man who talks about himself sets others talking, and there are deeds creditable to the doer that are best not spoken of. But I will tell you other things, and you   may draw your own conclusions.

"'Because Feisul refuses to attack the French, having promised those promise-breakers that he will not; and because Feisul has promised to protect the Jews and is likely to try to keep that promise to the promise-breaking English, certain of his intimates in Damascus, in whose confidence I am, have determined to force both issues, taking steps in his name that will commit him finally. Feisul's army of fifty thousand men is as ready as it will ever be. There is no money in the Damascus treasury, and therefore every moment of delay is now a moment lost. The time has come for action!'"

Our three prisoners were listening to the recitation spellbound, and so were we all for that matter. The mere memory feat was amazing enough. Few men could listen in hiding to a stranger's words, and report them exactly after an interval of more than an hour; but Narayan Singh did better than that, for he reproduced the speaker's gesture and inflexion, so that we had a mental picture of the scene that he described. Mabel offered him stewed tannic acid in the name of tea, and Ticknor suggested a chair, but he waved both offers aside and continued as if the picture before his mind and the words he was remembering might escape him if he took things easy.

"Sahib, they were very much excited when he spoke of action. First one man and then another stood up and boasted of having made all things ready; how this one had supervised the hiding of sharp swords; how another had kept men at work collecting cartridges on battlefields; how this and that one had continued spreading talk against the Jews, so that they swore that at least ten thousand Moslems in Jerusalem are fretting to begin a massacre. 'Let Feisul only strike the first blow from Damascus,' said they, 'and Palestine will run blood instantly!'"

"And we sit here drinking tea," exclaimed Mabel, "while up at headquarters they're dancing and playing bridge! I call this awful! We all ought to be..."

Grim smiled and shook his head for silence.

"We've known all this for some time," he said. "Don't worry. There'll be no massacre; the troops are sleeping by their arms, and every possible contingency has been provided for. Go on, Narayan Singh."

"Well, sahib; when they had done babbling and boasting this Yussuf Dakmar got back on his stool and spoke sternly, as one who gives final judgment and intends to be obeyed. 'It is we who must make the first move,' said he; 'and we shall force Feisul to move after us by moving in his name.' Whereat this man here, whose nose was broken on the fist of Jeremy sahib, said that a letter bearing Feisul's seal would make the matter easier. 'For the men,' said he, 'who are to slit Jews' throats will ask first for proof of our authority to bid them begin the business.'

"And at that speech Yussuf Dakmar laughed with great delight. 'Better late than never!' said he. 'Better to think of a wise precaution now than not at all! But oh, ye are an empty-headed crew!' he told them. 'I pity the conspiracy that had no better planning than ye would make for it without my fore thought! I thought of this long ago! I sent a message to Damascus, begging that a date be set and just such a letter sent to us. Feisul, I knew, would sign no such letter; but the paper he uses lies on an open desk, and there are men about him who have access to his seal. And because my appeal was well-timed it met with approval. A letter such as I asked for was written on Feisul's paper, sealed with his seal, and sent!'

"'But does it bear his signature?' a man asked.

"'How could it, since he never saw the letter?' Yussuf Dakmar answered.

"'Then few will pay heed to it,' said the other.

"'Perhaps if we were all such fools as you that might be so,' Yussuf Dakmar re-torted. 'However, fortunately the rest of us have readier wits! This letter is signed with a number, and the number is that of Feisul's generation in descent from the Prophet Mohammed. Let men be told that this is his secret signature, and when they see his seal beside it, will they not believe? Every hour in Jerusalem, and in all the world, men believe things less credible than that!'

"But at that, sahib, another man asked him how they might know that the letter really came from Damascus. 'It well might be,' said that one, 'a forgery contrived by Yussuf Dakmar himself, in which case though they might stir many Moslems into action by showing it, the men in Damascus would fail to follow up the massacre by striking at the French. And if they do not strike at the French,' said he, 'the French will not appeal to the British for aid; and so the British troops will be free to protect the Jews and butcher us, by which means we shall be worse off than before.'

"Whereat Yussuf Dakmar laughed again. 'If ye will go to the Sikh hospital,' said he, 'ye will find there the man who brought the letter. He lies in a cot in the upper storey with a knife-wound between his shoulder-blades. It was a mistaken accident unfortunate for him; the letter was intended for me, but I did not know that. What does the life of one fool matter? He gave out that Jews stabbed him, and it may be he believes that; yet I have the letter in my pocket here!' And he touched with one hand the portion of his coat beneath which was the pocket that contained the letter. I was watching, sahib, from where I lay hidden.

"He was about, I think, to show them the letter, when another thought occurred to him. He wrinkled his brow, as if seeking words in which to make his meaning clear, and they seemed willing enough to wait for him, but not so I, for I now knew where the letter was. So I sprang into their midst, falling less dangerously than I might have done by reason of a man's shoulders that served for a cushion. It may be that his bones broke under my weight. I can give no accurate report as to that, for I was in great haste. But as he gave way under me, I pitched forward, and, kicking Yussuf Dakmar in the belly with my boot, I fell on him, they falling on me in turn and we all writhing together in one mass on the floor. So I secured the letter."

"Good man!" Grim nodded.

"Wish I'd been there!" mourned Jeremy.

"And, having what I came for, I broke free; and taking the red stool I hurled it at the lamp, so that we were in total darkness, which made it a simple matter to unlock the door, and proceed about my business. Nevertheless, I heard them strike matches behind me, and it seemed unwise to take to my heels at once, it being easy to pursue a man who runs.

"As the sahib doubtless remembers, between that coffee shop and the next house is a stone buttress jutting out into the street, forming on its side farthest from the coffee-shop a dark corner, for whose filth and stink the street cleaners ought to be punished. Therein I lurked, while those who pursued ran past me up the street, I counting them; and among them I did not count Yussuf Dakmar and three more. It happened that a man was running up the street and the pursuers supposed him to be me. So I was left with only four to deal with; and it entered my head that no doubt Jimgrim sahib would be pleased to interview Yussuf Dakmar.

"And after a few moments Yussuf Dakmar came forth, and I heard him speak to these three fellows.

"'Those fools,' said he, 'hunt like street dogs at the sound of rubbish tossed out of a window. But I think that Indian soldier is less foolish than they. If I were he,' said Yussuf Dakmar, 'I think I wouldn't run far, with all these shadows to right and left and all the hours from now until dawn in which to act the fox. I suspect he is not far away at this minute. Nevertheless,' said he, 'those Indians are dangerous fellows. It is highly important that we get that letter from him; but it is almost equally important that we stop his mouth, which would be impossible if he should escape alive. If we wait here,' said he, 'we shall see him emerge from a shadow, if I am not much mistaken.'

"So they waited, sahib. And after a few minutes, when my breath had returned to me, I let him have credit as a wise one by emerging as he had said. And those four stalked me through the streets, not daring to come close until I should lead them to a lonely place; and I led them with discretion to this house, where happened what the sahib knows.

"That is all I know about this matter, except that being absent from duty on sick-leave there may be difficulty in the matter of my tunic, which is badly torn."

Having finished his story Narayan Singh stood at attention like one of those wooden images they used to keep on the sidewalk outside tobacco stores.

Grim smiled at the prisoners and asked whether they had any remarks to make--a totally lawless proceeding, for he did not caution them, and had no jurisdiction as a magistrate. They were three men caught red-handed attempting murder and burglary, and entitled accordingly to protection that the law doesn't always accord to honest men. But, as I have said, a true tale in the ears of criminals acts like a chemical reagent. It sets them to work lying, and the lie burns off, disclosing naked truth again. But, mother of me, they were daring liars! The fellow who had come out of the scrap more or less unscathed piped up for the three, the other two nodding and prompting him in whispers.

"What that Indian says in the main is true. He did jump down from the gallery and surprise a meeting summoned by Yussuf Dakmar. And it is true that Yussuf Dakmar's purpose is to bring about a massacre of Jews, which is to be simultaneous with an attack by Feisul's forces on the French in Syria. But we three men are not in favour of it. We have had no part in the preparations, although we know all details. We are honest men, who have the public interest at heart, and accordingly we have spied on Yussuf Dakmar, purposing to expose all his plans to the authorities."

Jeremy began humming to himself. Mabel tittered, and little Doctor Ticknor swore under his breath. But Grim looked as if he believed them --looked pleasantly surprised--and nodded gravely.

"But that hardly explains your following this Indian through the streets and attacking him on the veranda," he suggested, as if sure they could explain that too--as sure enough they did.

"We did not attack him. He attacked us. It was obvious to us from the first that he must be an agent of the Government. So when Yussuf Dakmar told us to follow and murder him we decided it was time to expose Yussuf Dakmar, and that this was our opportunity. We knew surely that this Indian would take that letter straight to some official of the Government; it was only necessary to pretend to hunt him and in that manner inveigle Yussuf Dakmar into the toils.

"But when we reached this house Yussuf Dakmar was afraid and refused to approach nearer than the street. He insisted on keeping watch outside the garden gate while we should draw near and shoot everyone who might be in the house and recover the letter. He is a coward, and we could not persuade him.

"So we decided to pretend to do his bidding, and to whisper through the window to the people within to pass out to the street by some back way and capture him, after which we would give all our evidence to the authorities.

"It was while we were looking through the window, seeking to call the attention of those within for that purpose and no other, that we were attacked and submitted to much unnecessary violence. That is the whole truth, as Allah is our witness! We are honest men, who seek to uphold the law, and we claim the protection of the Government. We are ready to tell all we know, including the names of those connected with this plot."

# CHAPTER V

"Nobody will know, no bouquets"

There followed a tedious hour or two, during which Grim cross-examined the three "honest men," and took down lists of names from their dictation, getting Doctor Ticknor meanwhile to go for the police because Yussuf Dakmar might still be lurking in the neighbourhood for a chance to murder Narayan Singh. It was only after the police had carried off the prisoners to jail (where they repudiated their entire confession next morning) that Grim showed us the letter which, like a spark, had fired a powder magazine--although a smaller one than its writer intended.

"It isn't in Feisul's handwriting," he said, holding the feathery Arab script up to the lamplight; "and it's no more like his phraseology than a camel resembles a locomotive. Listen to this:

To the Pan-Arab Committee in Jerusalem, by favour of Yussuf Dakmar Bey its District President, Greeting in the name of God:

Ye know that on former occasions the foes of our land and race were overwhelmed when, relying on the aid of the Most High, and raising the green banner of the Prophet--on whom be peace--we launched our squadrons in a cause held sacred by us all.

Ye know that in that fashion, and not otherwise, the accursed conquerors were driven forth and our sacred banner was set on high over the Damascus roofs, where by Allah's blessing may it wave for ever!

Ye know how those who claimed to be our friends have since proven themselves foes, so that the independent state for which we fought is held today in ignominious subjection by aliens, who deny the true Faith and hold their promises as nothing.

Ye know how Damascus is beset by the French, and Palestine is held by the British who, notwithstanding the oath they swore to us, are daily betraying us Arabs to the Jews.

Know now, then, that the hour has struck when, again in the name of Allah, we must finish what we formerly began and with our true swords force these infidels to yield our country to us. Nor on this occasion shall we sheathe our swords until from end to end our land is free and united under one government of our own choosing.

Know that this time there shall be no half-measures nor any compromise. It is written, Ye shall show no quarter to the infidel. Let no Jew live to boast that he has footing in the land of our ancestors. Leave ye no root of them in the earth nor seedling that can spring into a tree! Smite, and smite swiftly in the name of Him who never sleeps, who keeps all promises, whose almighty hand is ready to preserve the Faithful.

Whereunto ye are bidden to take courage. Whereunto our army of Syria stands ready. Whereunto the day has been appointed.

Know ye that the tenth day from the sending of this letter, and at dawn, is the appointed time. Therefore let all make common cause for the favour of the Most High which awaits the Faithful.

In the name of God and Mohammed the Prophet of God, on whom be blessings."

There followed the Moslem date and the numerical signature over Feisul's indubitable seal. Grim figured a moment and worked out the corresponding date according to our western calendar.

"Leaves six days," he said pleasantly. "It means the French intend to attack Damascus seven days from now."

"Let 'em!" Jeremy exploded. "Feisul'll give 'em ----! All they've got are Algerians."

"The French have poison gas," Grim answered dourly. "Feisul's men have no masks."

"Get 'em some!"

That was Jeremy again. Grim didn't answer, but went on talking:

"They're going to get Damascus.  All they've waited for was poison gas, and now there's no stopping 'em.  They forged this letter after the gas arrived.  Now if they catch Feisul in Damascus they'll put him on trial for his life, and they probably hope to get this letter back somehow to use as evidence against him."

"Go slow, Jim!" Mabel objected.  "Where's your proof that the French are jockeying this?  Isn't that Feisul's seal?"

"Yes, and it's his paper.  But not his handwriting."

"He might have dictated it, mightn't he?"

"Never in those words.  Feisul don't talk or write that way.  The letter's a manifest forgery, as I'll prove by confronting Feisul with it.  But there's a little oversight that should convince you it's a forgery.  Have you a magnifying glass, doc?"

Ticknor produced one in a minute, and Grim held the letter under the lamp.  On the rather wide margin, carefully rubbed out, but not so carefully that the indentation did not show, was the French word magnifique that had been written with a rather heavy hand and one of those hard pencils supplied to colonial governments by exporters from stocks that can't be sold at home.

"That proves nothing," Mabel insisted. "All educated Arabs talk French. Somebody on Feisul's staff was asked for an opinion on the letter before it went.  My husband's Arab orderly told me only yesterday that a sling I made for a man in the hospital was magnifique."

The objection was well enough taken, because it was the sort the forger of the letter would be likely to raise if brought to book. But Grim's argument was not exhausted.

"There are other points, Mabel.  For one thing, it's blue metallic ink. Feisul's private letters are all written with indelible black stuff made from pellets that I gave him;  they're imported from the States."

"But if Feisul wanted to prove an alibi, he naturally wouldn't use his special private ink," objected Mabel.

"Then why his seal, and his special private notepaper?  However, there's another point.  Feisul writes the purest kind of Arabic, and this isn't that sort of Arabic.  It was written by a foreigner--perhaps a Frenchman--possibly an Armenian--most likely a Turk--certainly one of the outer ring of politicians who have access to Feisul and seek to control him, but are not really in his confidence.  Damascus is simply a network of spies of that kind--men who attached themselves to the Arab cause when it looked like winning and are now busy transferring their allegiance.

"I think I could name the man who wrote this; I think I know the man who wrote that magnifique. If I'm right, Yussuf Dakmar will notify the French tonight through their agents in Jerusalem. The man who wrote that magnifique will know before morning that the letter's missing; and it doesn't matter how careful I may be, it'll be known as soon as I start for Damascus.

"They'll dope out that our obvious course would be to confront Feisul with this letter. The only way to travel is by train; the roads are rotten--in fact, no auto could get through; they'd tip off the Bedouins, who'd murder everybody.

"So they'll watch the trains and especially Haifa, where everyone going north has to spend the night; and they'll stop at nothing to get the letter back, for two reasons; as long as it's in our hands it can be used to establish proof of the plot against Feisul; once it's back in theirs, they can keep it in their secret dossier to use against Feisul if they ever catch him and bring him to trial. You remember the Dreyfus case?

"I shall start for Damascus by the early train--probably take an auto as far as Ludd. If I want to live until I reach Damascus I shall have to prove conclusively that I haven't that letter with me. Anyone known to be in British service is going to be suspected and, if not murdered, robbed. Ramsden has been seen about too much with me. Jeremy might juggle by but he's already notorious, and these people are shrewd. Better hold Jeremy in reserve, and the same with Narayan Singh. A woman's best. How about you, Mabel?"

"What d'you mean, Jim?"

"Do you know a woman in Haifa?"

"Of course I do."

"Well enough to expect a bed for the night at a moment's notice?"

"Certainly."

Mabel's eyes were growing very bright indeed. It was her husband who looked alarmed.

"Well, now, here's the point."

Grim leaned back in his chair and lit a cigarette, not looking at anybody, stating his case impersonally, as it were, which is much the shrewdest way of being personal.

"Feisul's up against it, and he's the best man in all this land, bar none. They've dealt to him from a cold deck, and he's bound to lose this hand whichever way he plays it. To put it differently, he's in check, but not checkmated. He'll be checkmated, though, if the French ever lay hands on him, and then good-bye to the Arab's chance for twenty years.

"I propose to save him for another effort, and the only way to do that is to convince him. The best way to convince him is to show him that letter, which can't be done if Feisul's enemies discover who carries it. If Ramsden, Jeremy, Narayan Singh and I start for Damascus, pretending that one or other of us has the letter concealed on his person, and if a woman really carries it, we'll manage. Is Mabel Ticknor going to be the woman? That's the point."

"Too dangerous, Jim! Too dangerous!" Ticknor put in nervously.

"Pardon me, old man. The danger is for us four, who pretend we've got the thing."

"There are lots of other women and I've only got one wife!" objected Ticknor.

"We're pressed for time," Grim answered. "You see, Ticknor, old man, you're a Cornstalk and therefore an outsider--just a medico, who saws bones for a living, satisfied to keep your body out of the poorhouse, your soul out of hell, and your name out of the newspapers. Your wife is presumably more so. There are several officials' wives who would jump at the chance to be useful; but a sudden trip toward Damascus just now would cause any one of them to be suspected, whereas Mabel wouldn't be."

"I don't know why not!" Ticknor retorted. "Wasn't she in here when those three murderers came to finish the lot of us? If Yussuf Dakmar makes any report at all he'll surely say he traced the letter to this house."

"Yussuf Dakmar came no nearer than the street," Grim answered. "He has no notion who is in here. His three friends are in jail under lock and key, where he can't get at them. How long have you had this house? Since yesterday, isn't it? D'you kid yourself that Yussuf Dakmar knows who lives here?"

"I can get leave of absence. Suppose I go in Mabel's place?" suggested Ticknor, visibly worried.

"The mere fact that she goes, while you stay here, will be presumptive evidence that she isn't on a dangerous mission," Grim answered. "No. It has got to be a woman. If Mabel won't go I'll find someone else."

You could tell by Mabel's eyes and attitude that she was what the salesmen call "sold" already; but you didn't need a magnifying glass to detect that Ticknor wasn't. Men of his wandering habit know too well what a brave, good-tempered wife means to encourage her to take long chances; for although there are lots of women who would like to wander and accept the world's pot luck, there are precious few capable of doing it without doubling a fellow's trouble; when they know how to halve the trouble and double the fun they're priceless.

Grim played his usual game, which is to spank down his ace of trumps face upward on the table. Most of us forget what are trumps in a crisis.

"I guess it's up to you, doc," he said, turning toward Ticknor. "There's nothing in it for you. Feisul isn't on the make; I don't believe he cares ten cents who is to be the nominal ruler of the Arabs, provided they get their promised independence. He'd rather retire and live privately. But he only considers himself in so far as he can serve the Arab cause. Now, you've risked Mabel's life a score of times in order to help sick men in mining camps, and malaria victims and Lord knows what else. Here's a chance to do the biggest thing of all--"

"Of course, if you put it that way..." said Ticknor, hesitating.

"Just your style too. Nobody will know. No bouquets. You won't have to stammer a speech at any dinner given in your honor."

"D'you want to do it, Mabel?" asked Ticknor, looking at her keenly across the table.

"Of course I do!"

"All right, girl. Only, hurry back."

He looked hard at Grim again, then into my eyes and then Jeremy's.

"She's in your hands. I don't want to see any of you three chaps alive again unless she comes back safe. Is that clear?"

"Clear and clean!" exploded Jeremy. "It's a bet, doc. Half a mo', you chaps; that's my mine at Abu Kem, isn't it? I've agreed to give the thing to Feisul and make what terms I can with him. Jim and Rammy divvy up with me on my end, if any. That right? I say; let the doc and Mabel have a half-share each of anything our end amounts to."

Well, it took about as long to settle that business as you'd expect. The doctor and Mabel protested, but it's easier to give away a fortune that is still in prospect than a small sum that is really tangible--I mean between folk who stand on their own feet. It doesn't seem to deprive the giver of much, or to strain the pride of the recipient unduly.

I've been given shares in unproven El Doradoes times out of number, and could paper the wall of, say, a good-sized bathroom with the stock certificates--may do it some day if I ever settle down. But the only gift of that sort that I ever knew to pay dividends, except to the printer of the gilt-edged scrip, is Jeremy's gold mine; and you'll look in vain for any mention of that in the stock exchange lists. The time to get in on that good thing was that night by Mabel Ticknor's teapot in Jerusalem.

It was nearly midnight before we had everything settled, and there was still a lot to do before we could catch the morning train. One thing that Grim did was to take gum and paper and contrive an envelope that looked in the dark sufficiently like the alleged Feisul letter; and he carried that in his hand as he took to the street, with Narayan Singh following among the shadows within hail. Jeremy and I kept Narayan Singh in sight, for it was possible that Yussuf Dakmar had gathered a gang to waylay whoever might emerge from the house.

But he seemed to have had enough of bungling accomplices that night. Grim hadn't gone fifty paces, keeping well in the middle of the road, when a solitary shadow began stalking him, and doing it so cautiously that though he had to cross the circles of street lamplight now and then neither Jeremy nor I could have identified him afterward.

Narayan Singh had orders not to do anything but guard Grim against assault, for Grim judged it wise to leave Yussuf Dakmar at large than to precipitate a climax by arresting him. He had the names of most of the local conspirators, and if the leader were seized too soon the equally dangerous rank and file might scatter and escape.

Down inside the Jaffa Gate, in a dark alley beside the Grand Hotel, there are usually two or three cabs standing at any hour of the night ready to care for belated Christian gentlemen who have looked on the wine when it was any colour that it chanced to be. There were three there, and Grim took the first one, flourishing his envelope carelessly under the corner lamp.

Yussuf Dakmar took the next in line, and ordered the driver to follow Grim. So we naturally took the last one, all three of us crowding on to the rear seat in order to watch the cabs in front. But as soon as we had driven back outside the city gate Yussuf Dakmar looked behind him and, growing suspicious of us, ordered his driver to let us pass.

It would have been too obvious if we had stopped too, so we hid our faces as we passed, and then put Jeremy on the front seat, he looking like an Arab and being most unrecognizable. Yussuf Dakmar followed us at long range, and as the lean horses toiled slowly up the Mount of Olives to headquarters the interval between the cabs grew greater. By the time we reached the guard-house and answered the Sikh sentry's challenge there was no sign of Grim in front, and we could only hear in the distance behind us the occasional click of a loose shoe to tell that Yussuf Dakmar was still following.

# CHAPTER VI

"Better the evil that we know..."

Yussuf Dakmar had his nerve with him that night, or possibly desperation robbed him of discretion. He may have been a more than usually daring man with his wits about him, but you'd have to hunt down the valley of death before you could bring the psychoanalytic guns to bear on him for what they're worth. I can only tell you what he did, not why he did it.

The great hospice that the German nation built on the crown of the Mount of Olives to glorify their Kaiser stood like a shadow among shadows in its compound, surrounded by a fairly high wall. There was a pretty strong' guard under an Indian officer in the guard-house at the arched main gate where the sentry challenged us.

A sentry stood at the foot of the steps under the portico at the main entrance, and there was another armed man on duty patrolling the grounds. But there were one or two other entrances, locked, though quite easy to negotiate, which the sentry could only observe while he marched toward them; for five minutes at a time, while his back was turned, at least two gates leading to official residences offered opportunity to an active man.

One lone light at a window on the top floor suggested that the officer of the night might be awake, but what with the screeching of owls and a wind that sighed among the shrubs, headquarters looked and sounded more like a deserted ancient castle than the cranium and brain-cells of Administration.

We heard Yussuf Dakmar stop his cab two hundred yards away. The cabman turned his horses and drove back toward Jerusalem without calling on Allah to witness that his fare should have been twice what he received; he didn't even lash the horses savagely; so we supposed that he hadn't been paid, and went on to deduce from that that Yussuf Dakmar had driven away again, after satisfying himself that the Feisul letter had reached headquarters. It was lazy, bad reasoning--the sort of superficial, smart stuff that has cost the lives of thousands of good men times out of number--four o'clock o' the morning intelligence that, like the courage of that hour, needs priming by the foreman, or the sergeant-major, or the bosun as the case may be.

The sentry turned out the guard, who let us through the gate after a word with Narayan Singh; and the man who leaned on his bayonet under the portico at the end of the drive admitted us without any argument at all.

I suppose he thought that having come that far we must be people in authority. Ever since then I have believed all the stories told me about spies who walked where they chose unchallenged during wartime; for we three--a Sikh enlisted man, an Australian disguised as an Arab, and an American in civilian clothes--entered unannounced and unwatched the building where every secret of the Near East was pigeonholed.

We walked about the corridors and up and downstairs for ten minutes, looking in vain for Grim. Here and there a servant snored on a mat in a corner, and once a big dog came and sniffed at us without making any further comment. Jeremy kicked one man awake, who, mistaking him for an Arab, cursed him in three languages, in the name of three separate gods, and promptly went to sleep again. The sensation was like being turned loose in the strong-room of a national treasury with nobody watching if you should choose to help yourself. There are acres of floor in that building. We walked twice the whole circuit of the upper and lower corridors, knocking on dozens of doors but getting no answer and finally brought up in the entrance hall.

Then it occurred to me that Grim might have gone into the building by some private entrance, perhaps round on the eastern side, so we set out to look for one.

We had just reached the northwest angle of the building, when Narayan Singh, who was walking a pace in front, stopped suddenly and held up both hands for silence. Whoever he could see among the shadows must have heard us, but it was no rare thing for officers to come roistering down those front steps and along the drive hours after midnight, and our sudden silence was more likely to give alarm than the noise had been. I began talking again in a normal voice, saying anything at all, peering about into the shadows meanwhile. But it was several seconds before I made out what the Sikh's keener eyes had detected instantly, and Jeremy saw it before I did.

There was a magnolia shrub about ten paces away from us, casting a shadow so deep that the ground it covered looked like a bottomless abyss. But nevertheless, something bright moved in it--perhaps the sheen of that lone light in an upper window reflected on a knife-hilt or a button--something that moved in time to a man's breathing.

If there was a certainty in the world it was that somebody who had no right to be there was lurking in that shadow, and he was presumably up to mischief. On the other hand, I had absolutely no right in that place either. Jeremy and Narayan Singh, being both in the British Army, were liable to be disciplined, and I might be requested to leave the country, if we should happen to blunder and tree the wrong 'possum, revenge being more than usually sweet to the official disturbed in the pursuit of unauthorized "diplomacy." It might even be some clandestine love affair.

So I took each of my companions by the arm, gripping Jeremy's particularly tightly, and started forward, whispering an explanation after we had turned the corner of the building. "Let one of us go and warn the guard," I suggested. "If we should draw that cover and start a shindy, we're more likely to get shot by the guard than thanked."

So Narayan Singh started off for the guard-house, he being the one most capable of explaining matters to the Sikh officer, and Jeremy and I crept back through the shadows to within earshot of the dark magnolia tree, choosing a point from which we could see if anybody bolted.

You know how some uncatalogued sense informs you in the dark of the movement of the man beside you? I looked suddenly sideways toward Jeremy, knowing, although I couldn't see him, that his eyes were seeking mine. It is only the animals who omit in the darkness those instinctive daylight movements; men don't have sufficient control of themselves. We had both heard Grim's voice at the same instant, speaking Arabic but unmistakable.

There were three men there. Grim was talking to the other two.

"Keep your hands on each other's shoulders! Don't move! I'm going to search all your pockets again. Now, Mr. Charkian. Ah! That feels like quite a pretty little weapon; mother o' pearl on the butt? Have you a permit? Never mind; not having the weapon you won't need a permit, will you? And papers--Mashallah! What a lot of documents; they must be highly important ones since you hide them under your shirt. I expect you planned to sell them, eh? Too bad! Too bad!

"You keep your hands on Mr. Charkian's shoulders, Yussuf Dakmar, or I'll have to use violence! I'm not sure, Mr. Charkian, that it wouldn't be kinder to society to send you to jail after all; you need a bath so badly. It seems a pity that a chief clerk to the Administration shouldn't have a chance to wash himself, doesn't it? Well, I'll have to read these papers afterward--after we've usurped the prerogative of Destiny and mapped out a little of the future. Now--are you both listening? Do you know who I am?"

There was no answer. "You, Mr. Charkian?"

"I think you are Major Grim."

"Ah! You wish to flatter me, don't you? Never mind; let us pretend I'm Major Grim disguised as an Arab; only, I'm afraid we must continue the conversation in Arabic; I might disillusion you if I tried to talk English. We'll say then that I'm Major Grim, disguised. Let's see now... What would he do in the circumstances? Here's Yussuf Dakmar, wanted for murder in the city and known to be plotting a massacre, seen climbing a wall when the sentry's back was turned, and caught in conference with Mr. Charkian, confidential clerk to the Administration. I'm sorry I didn't hear all that was said at your conference, for that might have made it easier to guess what Major Grim would do."

"Don't play with us like a cat playing with a mouse!" snarled somebody. "Tell us what you want. If you were Major Grim you'd have handed us over to those officers who passed just now. You're just as much irregular as we are. Hurry up and make your bargain, or the guard may come and arrest us all!"

"Yes, hurry up!" complained the other man. "I don't want to be caught here; and as for those papers you have taken, if we are caught I shall say you stole them from the office--you and Yussuf Dakmar, and that I followed you to recover them, and you both attacked me!"

"Very well," said Grim's voice pleasantly. "I'll let you go. I think you're dangerous. You'd better be quick, because I think I hear the guard coming!"

"Give me back the papers, then!"

"Aha! Will you wait and discuss them with the guard, or go at once?"

The Armenian clerk didn't answer, but got up and slunk away.

"Why did you let that fool go?" demanded Yussuf Dakmar. "Now he will awaken some officer and start hue and cry with a story that we robbed him. Listen! There comes the guard! We had better both run!"

"Not so fast!" Grim answered.

And then he raised his voice perceptibly, as if he wished to be overheard:

"I think those men who passed just now were not officers at all. Perhaps they were strangers. It may be that one of them is confused, and is leading the guard in the wrong direction!"

"Don't make so much noise then!" retorted Yussuf Dakmar. Jeremy, who thinks habitually about ten times as fast as I do, slipped away at once into the shadows to find Narayan Singh and decoy the guard elsewhere. I didn't envy him the job, for Sikhs use cold steel first and argue afterward when on the qui vive in the dark. However, he accomplished his purpose. Narayan Singh saved his life, and the guard arrested him on general principles. You could hear both Jeremy and Narayan Singh using Grim's name freely. Yussuf Dakmar wasn't deaf. He gave tongue:

"There! Did you hear that? They are speaking of Major Grim. You are a fool if you wait here any longer. That fellow Grim is a devil, I tell you. If he finds us we are both lost!"

"We have to be found first," Grim answered, and you could almost hear him smile.

"Quick then! What do you want?" snapped Yussuf Dakmar. Grim's answer was the real surprise of the evening. It bewildered me as much as it astonished Yussuf Dakmar.

"I want that letter that came from the Emir Feisul!"

"I haven't got it! I swear I haven't!"

"I know that already, for I searched you. Where is it?"

"Ask Allah! It was stolen by a Sikh, who delivered it to someone in a house near the military hospital, who in turn gave it to an Arab, who brought it here. I hoped that fellow Charkian might steal it back again, but you have spoiled everything. Charkian will turn against me now to save himself. What do you want with the letter?"

"I must have it!" Grim answered. "The French agent--"

"What--Sidi Said? You know him?"

"Surely. He would pay me a thousand pounds for it."

"May Allah change his face! He only offered me five hundred!"

"You have seen him already, then?" Grim asked. "I don't believe you! When did you see him?"

"On the way up here. He stopped my cab to speak to me at the foot of the hill."

I began to see the drift of Grim's purpose. He had established the fact that the French secret agent was already on the track of the letter, and that in turn explained why he had not seized Yussuf Dakmar and put him in jail. It was better to use the man, as the sequel proved. And Yussuf Dakmar walked straight into Grim's trap.

"What is your name?" he demanded.

"Call me Omar," said Grim.

"A Turk, are you? Well, Omar, let us help each other to get that letter, and divide the reward. Sidi Said told me that the British are sure to confront Feisul with it, and to do it secretly if they can. They will try to send it to Damascus. Let us two find out who takes it, and waylay him."

"Why should I divide with you?" demanded Grim, who is much too good an actor to pretend to agree without bargaining.

"Because otherwise you will not succeed. I was afraid of you when you first surprised me with Charkian. But now that I know you for a spy in the pay of the French I am not afraid of you, even though you have my revolver and dagger. You dare not kill me, for I would shout for help and the guard would come. You are in danger as much as I am. So you may either agree to work with me, sharing the reward, or you may work alone and have nothing for your pains; for I shall bring accomplices to help me take the letter from you after you have stolen it!"

Well, I suppose that anyone with criminal intentions could submit gracefully to that much blackmail. Besides, Grim was rather pressed for time and couldn't afford to prolong the argument.

"I see you are a determined man," he answered. "Your demand is unreasonable, but I must agree to it."

"Then give me back my pistol!"

"No. I need it. I lent mine this evening to another man, who has not yet returned it. That was a piece of wood with which I held you up just now. You must get yourself another."

"They are hard to come by in Jerusalem. Give me mine back."

"No. I shall keep it to protect myself against you."

"Why? You have no need to fear me if we work together."

"Because I intend to tell you what I know; and I may find it convenient to shoot you if you betray the information."

"Oh! Well, tell away."

"I have been cleverer than you," Grim announced blandly. "I knew who had given the order to the Sikh to steal that letter from you, and I was concealed in his house when the letter was brought to him. I heard the conference that followed, so I know what is going to be done about it."

"Oh! That was very smart. Well, tell me."

"Three men are going to take the letter to Damascus, but I don't know which of them will have it on his person. One is an Arab. One is an American. The third is that same Sikh who took the letter from you. They will take the train from Ludd, and I have engaged myself as servant to the American."

"Now that was extremely clever of, you!" said Yussuf Dakmar.

"Yes," Grim agreed. "But perhaps it will be as well to have an accomplice after all, and you will do as well as any. If I steal the letter they may accuse me; but if I can pass it to you, then I can submit to a search and oblige them to apologize."

"True! True! That will be excellent."

"So you had better take the morning train for Damascus," Grim continued. "But understand: If you bring others with you I shall suspect you of intending to play a trick on me. In that event I shall shoot you with your own pistol, and take my chance of escaping afterward. In fact, you are a dead man, Yussuf Dakmar, the minute I suspect you of playing me false."

"The same to you likewise!" Yussuf Dakmar answered fervently.

"Then we understand each other," said Grim. "The best thing you can do between now and train-time is to see the French agent again."

"What good will that do? He is irritable--nervous; he will only ask a thousand questions."

"Then your visit will do all the more good. You can calm him. We don't want a horde of fools interfering with us on the journey. We want to work quietly, and to share the reward between us. Therefore, you should tell him that you are confident of getting the letter if he will only leave the business to you alone. Give him every assurance, and explain to him that interference may mean failure. Now, I have done much the greater part so far; let this be your share to balance the account between us; you go to Sidi Said, the French agent, and make sure that he doesn't hinder us by trying to help."

"Very well, I will do that. And I shall meet you at the station in the morning?"

"No. My party will go as far as Ludd by motor. You will see us join the train there. Go now, while the guard is out of the way."

I could not see, but I heard Yussuf Dakmar get up and go. He had hardly time to get out of earshot when Grim's voice broke the silence again:

"You there, Ramsden?"

Instead of answering I approached.

"Did you hear what was said?" he asked.

"Yes. Why didn't you arrest both the blackguards and have done with it?"

"Better the evil that we know..." he answered, with the familiar smile in his voice. "The important thing is to sidetrack the French agent, who could put fifty ruffians on our trail instead of one."

"Why not send a provost-marshal's guard to the French agent, then?"

"Can't do that. France and Great Britain are allies. Besides, they might retaliate by spiflicating our agent in Damascus. Wise folk who live in glass-houses don't throw stones. What I think has been accomplished is to reduce our probable risk down to Yussuf Dakmar, who's a mean squib at best; and I think we've drawn suspicion clear away from Mabel Ticknor. All that remains is for me to go to that room where you see the light burning and discuss matters with the chief."

"If he's awake he's lonely!" said I; and I told Grim of our experience inside the building.

"Yes," he said. "Governments are all like that. They talk glibly of the ship of state; but a ship run in the same way would pile up or sink the first night out. You'd better go home and get an hour's sleep; I'll call you at seven."

"We'll take turns sleeping on the train," I answered. "Come first and rescue Jeremy. I think the guard pinched him. Say, did you intend one of us to go and decoy the guard away that time you raised your voice?"

"Sure. Recognized your voices--yours especially--when you passed, and heard you breathe as you crept back. You nearly spoilt the game by turning out the guard, but you saved it again handsomely."

"It's a marvel those Sikhs didn't shoot Jeremy in the dark," I answered.

"You bet it is," said Grim. "I guess he's too useful to be allowed to die just now."

He hung his head, thinking, as we walked side by side. "That was a close shave--too close! Well, as you say, let's go and rescue him."

---

# CHAPTER VII

"You talk like a madman!"

G rim changed the plan a little at the last minute. Mabel Ticknor left Jerusalem by train, as agreed, but Narayan Singh was sent that way too, to keep an eye on her. He being a Sikh, could sit in the corridor without exciting comment, and being dressed for the part of a more or less prosperous trader, he could travel first class without having to answer questions or allay suspicion.

Grim, Jeremy and I drove to Ludd in a hired auto, Grim and Jeremy both in Arab costume, and I trying to look like a tourist. Jeremy was supposed to be a travelled Arab intent on guiding me about Damascus for the usual consideration.

The platform was crowded, and we secured a compartment in the train without calling much attention to ourselves. There were British officers of all ranks, Egyptians, Jews, Greeks, refugee Armenians, Maltese, Kurds, a Turk or two, Circassians, men from as far off as Bokhara, Turkomans, Indians of all sorts, a sprinkling of Bedouins looking not quite so at home as in their native desert, and local Arabs by the score. About half of them were in a panic, encouraged to it by their shrill women-folk, fighting in a swarm for tickets at one small window, where an insolent Levantine demonstrated his capacity for self-determination by making as many people as possible miss the train. I caught sight of Mabel Ticknor in the front compartment of our car, and Grim pointed out Yussuf Dakmar leaning through a window of the car behind. His face was fat, unwholesome, with small, cold eyes, an immoral nose, and a small mouth with pouting lips. The tarboosh he wore tilted at an angle heightened the general effect of arrogant self-esteem. He was an illustration of the ancient mystery--how is it that a man with such a face, and such insolence written all over him, can become a leader of other men and persuade them to hatch the eggs of treachery that he lays like a cuckoo in their nests?

He smirked at Grim suggestively as we went by, and Grim, of course, smirked back, with a sidewise inclination of the head in my direction, whereat Yussuf Dakmar withdrew himself, apparently satisfied.

"Now he'll waste a lot of time investigating you," said Grim in an undertone. "We'd better keep awake in turns, or he'll knife you."

"The toe of my boot to him!" I retorted. "One clean kick might solve this international affair!"

"Steady!" Grim answered. "We need him until after leaving Haifa. The French agent wired, and they'll have a gang at Haifa ready for us; but Yussuf Dakmar will warn them off if we keep him hoping."

So we settled down into our compartment after a glance to make sure that Mabel was all right, and for about two minutes I imagined we were in for a lazy journey. Narayan Singh was on a camp-stool in the corridor, snoozing with one eye open like a faithful sheep-dog. It didn't seem possible for a creature like Yussuf Dakmar to make trouble for us, and I proposed that we should match coins for the first turn to go to sleep.

We had just pulled our coins out, and the engineer was backing the train in order to get her started, when Yussuf Dakmar arrived at our door, carrying his belongings, and claimed a seat on the strength of a lie about there being no room elsewhere.

There's something about a compartment on a train that makes whoever gets in first regard the rest of the world as intruders. Nobody would have been welcome, but we would have  preferred a pig to Yussuf Dakmar. Jeremy, democrat of democrats, who had slept without complaining between the legs of a dead horse on a rain-swept battlefield, with a lousy Turkish prisoner hugging him close to share the blanket, was up in arms at once.

"Imshi!" he ordered bluntly.

But Yussuf Dakmar was delighted. The reception convinced him, if anything were needed to do that, that one of us really was guarding the secret letter; and he was one of those hogs, anyhow, who glory in snouting in where they are plainly not wanted. He took the corner seat opposite Jeremy, tucked his legs up under him, produced a cigarette and smiled offensively. I'll concede this, though: I think the smile was meant to be ingratiating.

He pulled out a package wrapped in newspaper and began to eat before the train had run a mile. And, you know, more men get killed because of how they eat than by the stuff they devour. If you don't believe that, try living in camp for a week or two with a man who chews meat with his mouth open. You'll feel the promptings of a murderer. I know a scientist who swears that the real secret of the Cain and Abel story is that Abel sucked his gums at mealtime.

"You ought to be buried up to the neck and fed with a shovel!" Jeremy informed him in blunt English after listening to the solo for a while.

"Aha! That is the way they used to treat criminals in Persia," he answered pleasantly, with his mouth full of goat's milk cheese. "Only they put plaster of Paris in the hole, and when it rained the wretched man was squeezed until the blood came out of his mouth and eyes, and he died in agony. But how comes it that you speak to me in English? If we are both Arabs, why not talk the mother tongue?"

"My rump is my rump and the land is its rulers," Jeremy answered in Arabic, quoting the rudest proverb he could think of on the spur of the moment.

"Ah! And who is its ruler? Who is to be its ruler?"

Yussuf Dakmar made a surreptitious face at Grim, and his little cold eyes shone like a hungry pariah dog's. It began to be interesting to watch his opening gambit.

"I have heard tales," he went on, "of a new ruler for this country. What do you think of Feisul's chance?"

As he said that he eyed me sideways swiftly and keenly. Grim sat back in his own corner and folded up his legs, watching the game contentedly. Jeremy, intercepting Yussuf Dakmar's glance, put his own construction on it. He is a long, lean man, but like the Fat Boy in Pickwick Papers he likes to make your flesh creep, and humor, to have full zest for him, has to be mischievous.

So he commenced by pulling out his weapons one by one. The first was a razor, which he sharpened, tested with his thumb suggestively, and then placed in his sock, studying Yussuf Dakmar's throat for a minute or so after that, as if expecting to have to use the razor on it presently.

As the effect of that wore off he pulled out a pistol. It was one of the kind that won't go off unless you pull the Hammer back, but Yussuf Dakmar didn't know that, and if he had flesh and blood capable of creeping it's a safe assertion that they crept. Jeremy acted as if he didn't understand the weapon, and for fifteen minutes did more stunts with it than a puppy can do with a ball of twine. One of them that interested Yussuf Dakmar awfully was to point the pistol straight ahead, half-cocked, and try to get the hammer down by slapping it with the palm of his hand.

Most of our baggage was on the floor, but one fairly heavy valise was in the rack over Yussuf Dakmar's head. Jeremy got up to examine it when the pistol had ceased to amuse him, and taking advantage of a jerk as the train slowed down, contrived to drop it into the Syrian's lap; who rather naturally swore; whereat Jeremy took offence, and accused him of being a descendant of Hanna, son of Manna, who lived for a thousand and one years and never enjoyed himself.

It was our turn to eat sandwiches after that, while Yussuf Dakmar recovered from his disgruntlement. But just before the meal was finished Jeremy revived the game by asking suddenly in an awestruck whisper where "it" was. He slapped himself all over in a hurry, feeling for hidden pockets, and then came over and pretended to search me. There wasn't anything to do but fall in with his mood, so I resisted, searched my own pockets reluctantly, and said that we might as well take the next train back, since we had lost the important document.

Before we started we had put into a wallet the fake envelope that Grim had carried in his hand the previous night, and had entrusted the wallet to Jeremy in order to have an alibi ready for Mabel in case of need. Grim took up the cudgels now and reminded me respectfully, as a servant should when speaking to his master, that I had taken all proper precautions and could not be blamed in any event.

"But I think it will be found," he said hopefully. "Inshallah, it is not lost, but in the wallet in the pocket of that hare-brained friend of yours."

So Jeremy went back to his corner, searched for the wallet, found it after pretty nearly, standing on his head to shake his clothes, examined it excitedly, and produced the fake envelope, flourishing it so violently that nobody, even with eyes like a hawk's, could have identified it with certainty.

Then he dropped it in among the baggage on the floor, and went down on his knees to pick it up again. There is no more finished expert at sleight of hand than he, so it vanished, and he swore he couldn't find it. In a well-simulated agony of nervousness he called on Yussuf Dakmar to get down and help him search, and the

Syrian hadn't enough self-command left to pretend to hesitate; his cold eyes were nearly popping from his head as he knelt and groped. The chief subject of interest to me just then was how he proposed to retain the letter in the unlikely event of his finding it first.

It was a ridiculous search, because there wasn't really anywhere to look. After three bags had been lifted and their bottoms scrutinized the whole floor of the compartment lay naked to the eye, except where my feet rested. Jeremy insisted on my raising them, to the accompaniment of what he considered suitable comment on their size, turning his "behind end" meanwhile toward Yussuf Dakmar.

Grim chuckled and caught my eye. Yussuf Dakmar had walked straight into temptation, and was trying to search Jeremy's pockets from the rear--no easy matter, for he had to discover them first in the loose folds of the Arab costume.

Suddenly Jeremy's mood changed. He became suspicious, stood up, resumed his seat--and glared at Yussuf Dakmar, who retired into his corner and tried to seem unconscious of the game.

"I believe you are a thief--one of those light-fingered devils from El-Kalil!" said Jeremy suddenly, after about three minutes' silence. "I believe you have stolen my letter! Like the saint's ass, you are a clever devil, aren't you? Nevertheless, you are like a man without fingernails, whose scratching does him no good! Your labour was in vain. Give me back the letter, or by Allah I will turn you upside down!"

Yussuf Dakmar denied the accusation with all the fervour that a blackguard generally does use when, for once, he is consciously innocent.

"By the Beard of the Prophet and on my honor I swear to you that I haven't touched your letter! I don't know where it is."

"Show me the Prophet's beard!" commanded Jeremy. "Show me your honor!"

"You talk like a madman! How can I show either?"

"Then how can you swear by them? Father of easy words and evil deeds, give me the letter back!"

Yussuf Dakmar appealed to me as presumably responsible for Jeremy.

"You saw, effendi, didn't you? I tried to help him. But he who plays with the cat must suffer her claws, so now he accuses me of stealing. I call you to witness that I took nothing."

"You must excuse him," I answered. "That is a highly important letter. If it isn't found the consequences may be disastrous."

"By Allah, it shall be found!" exploded Jeremy, glaring harder than ever at Yussuf Dakmar. "Look at his face! Look at his evil eyes! He came in here on purpose to spy on us and steal that letter! It is time to use my razor on him! I swear not by the Prophet's beard or anybody's honor, but by the razor in my sock that he has the letter and that I will have it back!" Well, that was a challenge there was no sidestepping. Sure of being able to prove innocence, Yussuf Dakmar decided that a bold course was the best. He proceeded to empty his own pocket, laying the contents on the seat before Jeremy's eyes. And Jeremy watched like a puzzled puppy with his brow wrinkled. The process took time, because he was wearing one of those imitation Western suits, of prehistoric cut but up-to-date with every imaginable pocket that a tailor could invent. Their contents included a dagger and a clasp-knife with a long blade sharpened on both edges, but no pistol.

"Now are you satisfied?" he demanded, after turning inside-out the two "secret" pockets in the lining of his vest.

"Less than ever!" Jeremy retorted. "Until I see you naked I will not believe you!"

Yussuf Dakmar turned to me again. He was a patient spy, if ever there was one.

"Do you think I should be put to that indignity?" he asked. "Shall I undress myself?"

"By Allah, unless you do it I will cut your clothes off with my razor!" Jeremy announced.

We drew up at a station then, and had to wait until the train went on again. By that time Yussuf Dakmar had made up his mind. He slipped off his jacket and vest and began to unfasten his collar-button as the train gained speed.

Everything went smoothly until he stood up to remove his pants. He had the top of them in both hands when Jeremy seized him suddenly by the elbows and spun him face about. And there the letter lay, face downward on the seat he had just left, bent and a little crinkled in proof that he had been sitting on it for some minutes past.

Now it doesn't make any difference whether a man meant to take off his trousers or not. In a crisis, if they are unfastened, he will hold them up. It's like catching a monkey; you put corn into a narrow-necked basket. The monkey inserts his arm, fills his hand with corn, and tries to pull it out, but can't unless he lets go of the corn, which he won't do. So you catch him. Yussuf Dakmar held up his pants with one hand, and tried to free himself from Jeremy with the other. If he had let go his pants he might have seized the envelope and discovered what a fake it was; but he wouldn't do that. It was I who pounced on it and stowed it away carefully in my inner pocket.

Yussuf Dakmar's emotions were poignant and mixed, but he was no quitter. He thought he knew definitely where the letter was now, and the wolf glance with which he favoured me changed swiftly to a smile of ingratiating politeness.

"I am glad you have recovered what you lost," he said, smiling, as he fastened up his pants and resumed his coat. "This friend of yours--or is he your servant?--made me nervous with his threats, or I should certainly have found it for you sooner."

And now Grim resumed a hand. The last thing he wished was that Yussuf Dakmar should consider his quest too difficult, for then he would probably summon assistance at Haifa. Encouragement was the proper cue, now that Jeremy had tantalized him with a glimpse of the bait. We had nothing to fear from him unless he should lose heart.

"The value of a sum lies in the answer," he said, quoting one of those copybook proverbs with which all Syrians love to clinch an argument.

"The letter is in its owner's pocket. The accuser should now apologize, and we can spend the rest of the journey pleasantly."

Jeremy proceeded to apologize:

"So you're not such a thief as you looks."

Then he provided entertainment. He drew out the razor and did stunts with it, juggling it with open blade from hand to hand--pretending to drop it and always catching it again within a fraction of an inch of Yussuf Dakmar's person. By and by he juggled with coins, match-box, cigars, razor and anything he could lay his hands on.

"Mashallah!" exclaimed the Syrian at last, his face all sweaty with excitement as he shrank back to avoid the spinning razor. "Where did you learn such accomplishments?"

"Learn them?" answered Jeremy, still juggling. "I am a dervaish. I was born, not taught. I can ride through the air on cannon-balls, and whatever I wish for is mine the next minute. Look, I have one piastre. I wish for twenty. What do I do? I spin it in the air--catch it--d'you hear them? There you are--twenty! Count 'em if you like."

"A dervaish? A holy person? You? Where do you come from?"

"I was born in the belly of the South Wind," answered Jeremy. "Where I come from, every shell-fish has a pearl in it and gold is so common that the cattle wear it in their teeth. I can talk three languages at once and swear in six, use sulphur for tobacco, eat sardines without opening the can, and flavour my food for choice with gun-powder.

"I've been everywhere, seen everything, heard all the lies, and I found that big effendi in Jerusalem. I saw him first. He calls himself Ramsden, which is derived from the name of a creature bearing wool, which in turn is a synonym for money. He's on his way to supply Feisul with money, and I'm going to show him the streets of Damascus. Anything else you want to know?"

"Supply Feisul with money? That is interesting. American money perhaps? An American banker by any chance?"

"Nothing to do with chance. He's a father of certainties. Didn't he give me that letter to keep, and didn't I find a safe place for it between you and the cushions? Yes, I put it there. I'm an honest man, but I have my reasonable doubts about this other fellow. Ramsden effendi found him somewhere, and engaged him as a servant without asking me. Perhaps he's honest. Only Allah knows men's hearts. But he hasn't got an honest face like yours, and when pay-day comes I shall hide my money."

"So you know Damascus?" answered Yussuf Dakmar. "I hope you will come and see me in Damascus. I will give you my address. If Ramsden effendi has only engaged you temporarily, perhaps I can show you a way to make money with those accomplishments of yours."

"Make money?" answered Jeremy, prattling away like a madman. "I am weary of the stuff. I'm hunting the world over, in search of a friend. Nobody loves me. I want to find someone who'll believe the lies I tell him without expecting me to believe the truth he tries to foist on me. I want to find a man as tricky with his brains as I am with my hands. He must be a politician and a spy, because I love excitement.

That's why I called you a spy. If you were one, you might have admitted it, and then we could have been friends, like two yolks in one eggshell. But I see you're only a shell without a yolk in it. Who cleaned you?"

"How long have you been in the service of Ramsden effendi?" Yussuf Dakmar asked him.

"Not long, and I am tired of it. He is strong, and his fist is heavy. When he gets drunk he is difficult to carry upstairs to bed, and if I am also drunk the feat is still more difficult. It is a mystery how such a man as he should be entrusted with a secret mission, for he drinks with anyone. Aha! He scowls at me because I tell the truth about him, but if I had a bottle of whisky to offer him he would soon look pleasant again, and would give me a drink too, when he had swallowed all he could hold."

If he had really been my servant I would naturally have kicked him off the train for a fraction of such impudence. I didn't exactly know what to do. There is a thoughtful motive behind every apparently random absurdity that Jeremy gets off, but I was uncomfortably conscious of the fact that my wits don't work fast enough to follow such volatile manoeuvres. Perhaps it's the Scotian blood in me. I can follow a practical argument fast enough, when the axioms' are all laid down and we're agreed on the subject.

However, Grim came to my rescue. He had his pencil out, and contrived to flick a piece of paper into my lap unseen by Yussuf Dakmar.

Jeremy's cue is good [the note ran]. Dismiss him for talking about you to a stranger. Trust him to do the rest.

So I acted the part of an habitually heavy drinker in a fit of sudden rage, and dismissed Jeremy from my service on the spot.

"Very well," he answered blandly. "Allah makes all things easy. Let us hope that other fellow finds it easy to put you to bed tonight! Allah is likewise good, for I have my ticket to Damascus, and all I need to beg for is a bed and food at Haifa."

I muttered something in reply about his impudence, and the conversation ceased abruptly. But at the end of ten minutes or so Yussuf Dakmar went out into the corridor, signaling to Jeremy to follow him.

# CHAPTER VIII

"He'll forgive anyone who brings him whiskey."

You remember, of course, that line that Shakespeare put into the mouth of Puck? "What fools these mortals be!" The biggest fools are the extra smart ones, whose pride and peculiar joy it is to "beat the game."

Yussuf Dakmar assessed all other humans as grist for his mill. Character to him was expressed in degrees of folly and sheer badness. Virtue existed only as a weakness to be exploited. The question that always exercised him was, wherein does the other fellow's weakness lie? It's a form of madness. Where a sane man looks for strength and honesty that he can yoke up with, a Yussuf Dakmar spies out human failings; and whereas most of us in our day have mistaken pyrites for fine gold, which did not hurt more than was good for us, he ends by mistaking gold for dross.

You can persuade such a man without the slightest difficulty that you are a fool and a crook. Jeremy had turned the trick for his own amusement as much as anything, although his natural vein of shrewdness probably suggested the idea. Yussuf Dakmar, ready to believe all evil and no good of anyone, was convinced that he had to deal with a scatter- brained Arab who could be used for almost any purpose, and Jeremy's riotous bent for jumping from one thing to another fixed the delusion still more firmly.

But Lord, he had caught a Tartar! Outside at the end of the corridor, in full view, but out of earshot, of Narayan Singh, Yussuf Dakmar made a proposal to Jeremy that was almost perfect in its naive obliquity. There was nothing original or even unusual about it, except the circumstances, time and place. Green-goods men and blue-sky stock salesmen, race-course touts and sure-thing politicians get away with the same proposition in the U.S. every day of the week, and pocket millions by it. Only, just as happens to all such gentry on occasion, Yussuf Dakmar had the wrong fish in his net.

He jerked his head toward where Narayan Singh sat stolid and sleepy- looking on a camp-stool with his curly black beard resting on the heel of one hand.

"Do you know that man?" he asked.

"Wallah! How should I know him?" Jeremy answered. "He looks like a Hindu thinking of reincarnation. Inshallah, he will turn into a tiger presently!"

"Beware of him! He is an Administration spy. He is watching me talk to you, and perhaps he will ask you afterward what I have said. You must be very careful how you answer him."

"I will tell him you asked me for a love-potion for the engine-driver's wife," Jeremy answered.

"I am listening. What is it you are really going to say?"

"That master of yours--that Ramsden, who dismissed you so tyrannically just now--"

"That drunkard? There is nothing interesting to be said about him," Jeremy answered. "He is a fool who has paid my fare as far as Damascus. May Allah reward him for it!"

"Are you telling me the truth?" demanded Yussuf Dakmar, fixing his eyes sternly on Jeremy's.

Your con man never overlooks a chance to put his intended victim on the defensive at an early stage in the proceedings. "How can he have paid your fare as far as Damascus? This line only goes to Haifa, where you have to change trains and buy another ticket."

"I see you are a clever devil," Jeremy retorted. "May Allah give you a belly ache, if that is where you keep your brains! It was I who bought the tickets. The fool gave me sufficient money for three first-class fares all the way to Damascus, and I have the change. He forgot that when he dismissed me."

"Then you won't need to beg board and lodging in Haifa?"

"Oh, yes. I need my money for another matter. It is high time I married, and a fellow without money has to put up with any toothless
    that nobody else will take."

"So you hope to find a wife in Damascus?"

"Inshallah," Jeremy answered piously.

"Well, I will find you a good-looking girl for wife, provided you first prove that you will make a good son-in-law. I take men as I find them, not as they represent themselves. He who wishes for the fire must first chop wood. You understand me?"

"Wallah! I can chop wood like an axe with two heads. Is the woman your daughter?"

"That is as may be. Let us talk business. I reward my friends, but woe betide the fool who betrays my confidence!" said Yussuf Dakmar darkly.

"I see you are a man after my own heart," answered Jeremy; "a thorough fellow who stops at nothing! Good! Allah must have brought us two together for an evil purpose, being doubtless weary of the League of Nations; Unbosom! I am like a well, into which men drop things and never see them any more."

"You are a fine rascal, I can see that clearly! So you think that Allah is cooking up evil, do you? Tee-hee! That is an original idea, and there may be something in it. Let us hope there is something in it for us two, at all events. Now, as to that fellow Ramsden--"

"Avoid him unless he is drunk," advised Jeremy. "The weight of his fist would drive a man like you like a nail into a tree."

"Who fears such an ox?" the Syrian retorted. "A fly can sting him; a little knife can bleed him; a red rag can enrage him; and the crows who devour that sort of meat won't worry as to whether he was killed according to ritual! He has money for Feisul, has he? Well, never mind. He has a letter as well, and that is what I want. Will you get it for me?"

"Do you need it badly?"

"By Allah, I must have it!"

"By Allah, then I am in good luck, for that makes me indispensable, doesn't it? And an indispensable man can demand what he pleases!"

"Not at all," Yussuf Dakmar answered, frowning. "I have taken a fancy to you, or I would see you to the devil. When we reach Haifa, ten or even twenty men will present themselves to do this business for me. Or, if I choose, I can use that fellow Omar who is travelling with Ramsden; he would like to be my accomplice, but I don't trust him very much."

"In that you are perfectly right," answered Jeremy. "He is not at all the sort of man for you to trust. It wouldn't surprise me to learn that he has warned Ramsden against you already! Better beware of him!"

According to Jeremy's account of the conversation afterward, it was not until that moment that he saw clearly how to prevent Yussuf Dakmar from calling in thugs to attack me either at Haifa or at some point between there and Damascus. Until then he had been feeling his way along-- "spieling," as he calls it--keeping his man interested while he made all ready for the next trick.

"To tell you the truth," he went on, "Omar isn't that fellow's real name. He is a sharp one, and he is after the letter every bit as much as you are."

"How do you know that?"

"Wallah, how not? because he himself told me! just like you, he tried to get me into partnership. He offered me a big reward, but he's not like you, so I didn't believe him; and he has no daughter; I've no use for a man who hasn't a good-looking daughter. What he's afraid of is that someone else may get the letter first. And he's a desperate fellow. He told me his intentions and whether you believe me or not, they're worthy of a wolf!"

"I'm glad I resolved to take you into my confidence," said Yussuf Dakmar, nodding. "Go on; I'm listening. Tell me what he told you."

"He plans to get hold of the letter between Haifa and Damascus. He thinks that's safest, because it's over the border and there won't be any British officers to interfere. Somewhere up the Lebanon Valley, after most of the passengers have left the train, looks good to him. But I think he knows who you are."

"Yes, he knows me. Go on."

"And He's afraid you'll get help and forestall him. So he's going to watch Ramsden like a cat watching a mouse-hole, and he's going to watch you too. And if anybody tries to interfere at Haifa, or if men get on the train between Haifa and Damascus who look like being accomplices of yours, he's going to murder Ramsden there and then, seize the letter, and make a jump for it! You see, he's one of those mean fellows--a regular dog-in-the-manger; he'd rather get caught by the police and hanged for murder than let anybody else get what he's after. Oh, believe me, I didn't trust him! I laughed when he made his proposal to me."

"Now that is very interesting," said Yussuf Dakmar. "To tell you the truth I had a little experience with him last night myself. He came on me by accident in a certain place, and we conversed. I pretended to agree with him for the sake of appearances, but I formed a very poor opinion of him. Well, suppose we put him out of the way first; how would that be? You look like a strong man. Suppose you watch for an opportunity to push him off the train?"

"Oh, that would never do!" Jeremy answered, shaking his head from side to side. "You mustn't forget that Indian who sits in the corridor. It was you yourself who told me he is an Administration spy. If he suspects you already, he will suspect me for having talked with you, and will watch me; and if I try to push that fellow Omar off the train, he will come to the rescue. Surely you don't expect me to fight both of them at once! Besides, you must consider Ramsden.

"That fellow Ramsden is big and strong, but he is a nervous wreck. Give him the least excuse and he will yell for the police like a baby crying for its mother! He looks on Omar as his bodyguard now that he has dismissed me; and if Omar should get killed, or disappear between here and Haifa, Ramsden would demand an escort of police. In fact, I think he'd lose courage altogether and put that letter in a strongroom in the Haifa bank. What is the letter, anyway? What's in it? How much will you pay me if I get it for you?"

"Never mind what's in it. Will you get it, that's the point--will you get it and bring it to me?"

"That isn't the point at all," answered Jeremy. "The point is how much will you pay me if I do that?"

"Very well, I will pay you fifty pounds."

"Mashallah! You must need it awfully badly. I could have been hired for fifty shillings to do a much more dangerous thing!"

"Well, twenty-five pounds ought to be enough. I will pay you twenty- five."

"Nothing less than fifty!" Jeremy retorted. "I always get fifty of everything. Fifty lashes in the jail--fifty beans at meal-time--fifty pairs of boots to clean for Ramsden--fifty is my lucky number. I have made forty-nine attempts to get married, and the next time I shall succeed. If it isn't the woman's lucky number too, that's her affair. Show me the fifty pounds."

"I haven't that much with me," answered Yussuf Dakmar. "I will pay you in

Damascus."

"All right. Then I will give you the letter in Damascus."

"No, no! Get it as soon as possible."

"I will."

"And give it to me immediately. Then if you like you can stay close to me until I pay you in Damascus."

"'The ass is invited to a wedding to carry wood and water, and they beat him with one of the sticks he carried,'" Jeremy quoted. "No, no, no! I will get the letter, for I know how. After I have it you may keep close to me until we reach Damascus. I will show it to you, but I won't give it to you until after I get the fifty pounds."

"Very well, since you are so untrustful."

"Untrustful? I am possessed by a demon of mistrust! Why? Because I know I am not the worst person in the world, and what I can think of, another might do. Now, if you were I and I were you, which God forbid, because I am a happy fellow and you look bilious, and you stole the letter for me because I promised to pay you in Damascus, but wouldn't give me the letter until I paid you, do you know what I would think of doing? I would promise a few tough fellows ten pounds among them to murder you. Thus I would get the letter and save forty pounds."

"Ah? But I am not that kind of man," said Yussuf Dakmar.

"Well, you will learn what kind of man you are in the next world when you reach the Judgment Seat. What is most interesting now is the kind of fellow I am. I will steal the letter from Ramsden, and keep it until you pay me in Damascus. But I shan't sleep, and I shall watch you; and if I suspect you of making plans to have me robbed or murdered I shall make such a noise that everybody will come running, and then I shall be a celebrity but they'll put you in jail."

"Very well; you steal the letter, and I'll keep close to you," said Yussuf Dakmar. "But how are you going to do it, now that Ramsden has dismissed you from his service?"

"Oh, that's easy. You get me some whisky and I'll take it to him for a peace offering. He'll forgive anyone who brings him whisky."

"Tee-hee! That is quite an idea. Yes. Now--how can I get whisky on the train? If only I could get some! I have a little soporific in a paper packet that could be mixed with the whisky to make him sleep soundly. Wait here while I walk down the train and see what I can find."

Yussuf Dakmar was gone twenty minutes, and whether he begged, bought or stole did not transpire, but he returned with a pint flask containing stuff that looked and smelt enough like whisky to get by if there had been a label on the bottle. He poured a powder into it in Jeremy's presence, the two of them squatting on the floor of the corridor with the bottle between them so that no one else might see what was taking place.

"Now, you would better get rid of that fellow Omar while you attend to this," Yussuf Dakmar cautioned him. "Can you think of any way of doing that?"

"Oh, easily!" Jeremy answered. "He is a great one for the women. I will tell him there is a pretty Armenian girl in the car behind. He will run like any other Turk to have a good look at her."

"Very well. I will wait here. But understand now; I am a dangerous man. You have fortune in one hand, but destruction in the other!"

"Very well; but this may take me an hour, and if you grow impatient, and that Indian sees you peering into the compartment after having watched you and me talking all this time, he'll grow suspicious."

"All right; I'll go to the car behind. As soon as you have the letter, come and tell me."

So Jeremy came back and entertained Grim and me with a burlesque account of the interview, after whispering to Narayan Singh to give the alarm in the event of Yussuf Dakmar returning forward to spy on us. Grim put the doped whisky into his valise after a sniff at it, instead of throwing it out of the window at my suggestion; and after a suitable interval he went out in the part of the Turk to look for the imaginary beautiful Armenian. Then I gave Jeremy the fake letter back, and went to sleep.

So it's no use asking me what the country looks like between Ludd and Haifa. I didn't even wake up to see the Lake of Tiberias, Sea of Galilee, or Bahr Tubariya, as it is variously called. A rather common sickness is what Sir Richard Burton called Holylanditis and I've had it, as well as the croup and measles in my youth. Some folk never recover from it, and to them a rather ordinary sheet of water and ugly modern villages built on ruins look like the pictures that an opium smoker sees.

The ruins and the history do interest me, but you can't see them from the train, and after a night without sleep there seemed to me something more profitable in view than to hang from a window and buy fish that undoubtedly had once swum in Galilee water, but that cost a most unrighteous price and stank as if straight from a garbage heap.

The whole train reeked of putrid fish when we reached Haifa in the evening, in time to watch the sun go down across the really glorious Bay of Acre.

# CHAPTER IX

"The rest will be simple!"

Haifa was crowded with Syrians of all sorts, and there were two or three staff officers in the uniform of Feisul's army lounging on the platform, who conned new arrivals with a sort of childlike solicitude, as if by looking in a man's face they could judge whether he was friendly to their cause or not. Mabel had wired to her friend, and was met at the station, so we had nothing to worry over for the present on her score. Our own troubles began when we reached the only hotel and found it crowded. The proprietor, a little wizened, pockmarked Arab in a black alpaca jacket and yellow pants, with a tarboosh balanced forward at a pessimistic angle, suggested that there might be guests in the hotel who would let us share their beds...

"Although there will be no reduction of the price to either party in that event," he hastened to explain.

It was a wonder of an hotel. You could smell the bugs and the sanitary arrangements from the front-door step, and although the whole place had been lime-washed, dirt from all over the Near East was accumulating on the dead white, making it look leprous and depressing.

The place fronted on a main street, with its back toward the Bay of Acre at a point where scavengers used the beach for a dumping place. There was a hostel of British officers about a mile away, where Grim might have been able to procure beds for the whole party; but I noticed no less than five men who followed us up from the station and seemed to be keeping a watchful eye on Yussuf Dakmar and it was a sure bet that if we should show our hands so far as to mess with British officers, the train next day would be packed with men to whom murder would be simple amusement.

Yet Grim and Jeremy needed sleep and so did Narayan Singh. We offered to rent an outhouse for the night--a cellar--the roof, but there was nothing doing, and it was Yussuf Dakmar at last who solved the problem for us.

He found a crony of his, who had occupied for several days a room containing two beds. With unheard-of generosity, accompanied, however, by a peculiar display of yellow teeth and more of the jaundiced whites of his eyes than I cared to see, this individual offered to go elsewhere for the night and to place the room at my disposal.

"But there is this about it," he explained. "Where I am going there is no room for my friend Yussuf Dakmar Bey, so I must ask you to let him share this with you. You and he could each have a bed, of course, but it seems to me that your servants look wearier than you do. I suggest then that you take one bed, effendi, and share it with my friend Yussuf Dakmar Bey, leaving the other to your servants, who I hope will be suitably grateful for the consideration shown them."

Grim nodded to me from behind the Syrians' backs, and I jumped at the offer. Payment was refused. The man explained that he had the room by the week and the loan of it to me for one night would cost him nothing. In fact, he acted courteously and with considerable evidence of breeding, merely requesting my permission to lock the big closet where he kept his personal belongings and to take the key away with him. Even if we had been in a mood to cavil it would have been difficult to find fault, for it was a spacious, clean and airy room--three characteristics each of which is as scarce as the other in that part of the world.

The beds stood foot to foot along the right wall as you entered. Against the opposite wall was a cheap wooden wash-stand and an enormous closet built of olive wood sunk into a deep recess. The thing was about eight feet wide and reached to the ceiling; you couldn't tell the depth because he locked it at once and pocketed the key, and it fitted into the recess so neatly that a knife-blade would hardly have gone into the crack.

Outside the bedroom door, in a lobby furnished with odds and ends, was a wickerwork sofa that would do finely for Narayan Singh, and that old soldier didn't need to have it pointed out to him. Without word or sign from us he threw his kit on the floor, unrolled his blankets, removed his boots, curled up on the sofa, and if he didn't go to sleep at once, gave such a perfect imitation of it that somebody's fox terrier came and sniffed him, and, recognizing a campaigner after his own wandering heart, jumped on his chest and settled down to sleep too.

As soon as our host had left the room, all bows and toothy smiles, Jeremy with his back to me drew from one pocket the letter he was supposed to have stolen from me, flourished it in Yussuf Dakmar's face, and concealed it carefully in another. Then a new humorous notion occurred to him. He pulled it out again, folded it in the pocket wallet in which he had carried it from the first, wrapped the whole in a handkerchief, which he knotted carefully and then handed it to me.

"Effendi," he said, "you are a fierce master and a mighty drunkard, but a man without guile. Keep that till the morning. Then, if Omar wants to steal it he will have to murder you instead of me, and I would rather sleep than die. But you must give it back at dawn, because the prayers are in it that a very holy ma'lim wrote for me, and unless I read those prayers properly tomorrow's train will come to grief before we reach Damascus."

He acted the part perfectly of one of those half-witted, wholly shrewd mountebanks, who pick up a living by taking advantage of tolerance and good nature. You've all seen the type. It's commonest at race-meetings but you'll find it anywhere in the world where vagrant men of means foregather.

Again Yussuf Dakmar's face became a picture of suppressed emotion. I pocketed the wallet with the same matter-of-fact air with which I have accepted a servant's money to keep safe for him scores of times. He believed me to be a drunkard, who had been thoroughly doped that day and would probably drink hard that night to drown the after-taste. It ought to be easy to rob me while I slept. Any fool could have read his thoughts.

He came down and ate supper with us at a trestle table in the dimly lighted dining-room, and I encouraged his new-born optimism by ordering two bottles of whisky to take upstairs. Jeremy, who can't be happy unless playing his part for all it's worth, became devoutly religious and made a tremendous fuss because ham was put on the table. He accused the proprietor of using pig's fat to smear all the cooking utensils, demanded to see the kitchen, and finally refused to eat anything but leban, which is a sort of curds. If Yussuf Dakmar had entertained suspicions of Jeremy's real nationality they were all resolved by the time that meal was finished.

But the five' men who had followed us from the station sat in the dark at a table in the far corner of the room and watched every move we made. When the coffee was brought I sat smoking and surly over it, as if my head ached from the day's drink; Grim and Jeremy, aching for sleep but refusing like good artists to neglect a detail of their part, went to another table and played backgammon, betting quarrelsomely; and at last one of the five men walked over and touched Yussuf Dakmar's shoulder. At once he followed all five of them out of the room, whereat Grim and Jeremy promptly went to bed. It was so obviously my turn to stay awake that Grim didn't even trouble to remind me of it.

So I took the whisky upstairs, noticed that Narayan Singh was missing from the couch where he had gone to sleep, although the fox-terrier was snoring so loud in his blankets that I had to look twice in the dim light. I mentioned that fact to Grim who merely smiled as he got between the sheets. Then I went down to the street to get exercise and fresh air. I didn't go far, but strode up and down in front of the hotel a quarter of a mile or so in each direction, keeping in the middle of the street.

I had made the fourth or fifth turn when Narayan Singh came out and accosted me under the lamplight.

"Pardon," he called aloud in English, "does the sahib know where I can find a druggist's open at this hour? I have a toothache and need medicine."

"Come and I'll show you a place," said I with the patronizing air of a tourist showing off his knowledge, and we strode along together down the street, he holding one hand to his jaw.

"Thus and so it happened, sahib," he began as soon as we had gone a safe distance. "I lay sleeping, having kept my belly empty that I might wake easily. There came Yussuf Dakmar and five men brushing by me, and they all went into a room four doors beyond the sahib's. The room next beyond that one is occupied by an officer sahib, who fought at El-Arish alongside my battalion. Between him and me is a certain understanding based on past happenings in which we both had a hand. He is not as some other sahibs, but a man who opens both ears and his heart, and when I knocked on his door he opened it and recognized me.

"'Well?' said he. 'Why not come and see me in the morning?

"'Sahib,' said I, 'for the sake of El-Arish, let me in quickly, and close the door!'

"So he did, wondering and not pleased to be disturbed by a Sikh at such an hour.  And I said to him:

"'Sahib,' said I, 'am I a badmash?  A scoundrel?'

"'No,' said he, 'not unless you changed your morals when you left the service.'

"Said I, 'I am still in the service.'

"'Good,' said he. 'What then?'

"'I go listening again in no-man's land,' said I, and he whistled softly. 'Is there not a roof below your window?' I asked him, and he nodded.

"'Then let me use it, sahib, and return the same way presently.'

"So he threw back the shutter, asking no more questions, and I climbed out. The window of the room where Yussuf Dakmar and the five were stood open, but the lattice shutter was closed tight, so that I could stand up on the flat roof of the kitchen and listen without being seen.  And, sahib, I could recognize the snarl of Yussuf Dakmar's voice even before my ear was laid to the open lattice.  He was like a dog at bay.  The other five were angry with him.  They were accusing him of playing false.  They swore that a great sum could be had for that letter, which they should share between them.  Said a voice I did not recognize: 'If the French will pay one price they will pay another;  what does money matter to them, if they can make out a case against Feisul?  Will they not have Syria?  The thing is simple as twice two,' said he.  'The huntsman urges on the hounds, but unless he is cleverer than they, who eats the meat?  The French regard us as animals, I tell you!  Very well; let us live up to the part and hunt like animals, since he who has the name should have the game as well;  and when we have done the work and they want booty let them be made aware that animals must eat!  We will set our own price on that document.'

"'And as for this Yussuf Dakmar,' said another man, 'let him take a back seat unless he is willing to share and share alike with us.  He is not difficult to kill!'

"And at that, sahib, Yussuf Dakmar flew into a great rage and called them fools of complicated kinds.

"'Like hounds without a huntsman, ye will overrun the scent!' said he; and he spoke more like a man than any of them, although not as a man to be liked or trusted.  'Who are ye to clap your fat noses on the scent I found and tell me the how and whither of it?  It may be that I can get that letter tonight.  Surely I can get it between this place and Damascus;  and no one can do that, for I, and I only, know where it is. Nor will I tell!' And they answered all together, 'We will make you tell!'

"But he said, 'All that ye five fools can do is to interfere. Easy to kill me, is it? Well, perhaps. It has been tried. But, if so, then though ye are jackals, kites and vultures all in one with the skill of chemists added, ye can never extract secret knowledge from a dead man's brain. Then that letter will reach Feisul tomorrow night; and the French, who speak of you now as of animals, will call you what? Princes? Noblemen?'

"I suppose they saw the point of that, sahib, for they changed their tone without, however, becoming friendly to Yussuf Dakmar. Thieves of that sort know one another, and trust none, and it is all a lie, sahib, about there being any honor among them. Fear is the only tie that binds thieves, and they proceeded to make Yussuf Dakmar afraid.

"There seems to be one among them, sahib, who is leader. He has a thin voice like a eunuch's, and unlike the others swears seldom.

"This father of a thin voice accepted the situation. He said: "'Well and good. Let Yussuf Dakmar do the hunting for us. It is sufficient that we hunt Yussuf Dakmar. Two of us occupy the room next to Ramsden's. If Yussuf Dakmar needs aid in the night, let him summon us by scratching with his nails on the closet door. The rest will be simple. There are four in this besides us five; so if we count Yussuf Dakmar that makes ten who share the reward. Shall Yussuf Dakmar grow fat, while nine of us starve? I think not! Let him get the letter, and give it to me. We will hide it, and I will deal with the French. If he fails tonight, let him try again tomorrow on the train. But we five will also take that train to Damascus, and unless that letter is in my hands before the journey's end, then Yussuf Dakmar dies. Is that agreed?'

"All except Yussuf Dakmar agreed to it. He was very angry and called them leeches, whereat they laughed, saying that leeches only suck enough and then fall off, whereas they would take all or kill. They made him understand it, taking a great oath together to slay him without mercy unless he should get the letter and give it to them before the train reaches Damascus tomorrow evening.

"Well, sahib, he agreed presently, not with any effort at good grace, but cursing while he yielded.

"In truth, sahib, it is less fear than lack of sleep that Yussuf Dakmar feels. I could hear him yawn through the window lattice. Now a man in that condition is likely to act early in the night for fear that sleep may otherwise get the better of him, and the sahib will do well to be keenly alert from the first. I shall be asleep on that couch outside the door and will come if called, so the sahib would better not lock the door but should call loud in case of need, because I also have been long awake and may sleep heavily."

"Suppose I walk the streets all night?" said I. "Wouldn't that foil them?"

"Nay, sahib, but the reverse; for if Yussuf Dakmar should miss you after midnight he would go in search of you, with those five in turn tracking him. And as for finding you, that would be a simple matter, for every night thief and beggar waiting for the dawn would give attention to such a big man as you and would report your movements. All six would come on you in the dark and would kill you surely. Then, as if that were not bad enough, having searched you they would learn that the letter in your possession is not the right one; and the trail of the right one would be that much easier to detect."

"Then come with me," said I, "and we'll make a night of it together. You and I can defend ourselves against those six."

"Doubtless, sahib. But my place is within hail of Jimgrim. No, it is best that you see this matter through tonight between four walls. Only remember, sahib, that though a man on duty may feign sleep, it is wiser not to, because sleep steals on us unawares!"

So I returned to the bedroom where Grim and Jeremy were snoring a halleluja chorus; but Yussuf Dakmar hadn't returned yet. I took advantage of the Syrian's absence to open Grim's valise, remove the bottle of doped whisky and set it on the table close to the window beside the two bottles that I had bought downstairs--one of which, for the sake of appearances, I opened just as Yussuf Dakmar entered, smiling to conceal anxiety.

## CHAPTER X

"You made a bad break that time"

G rim was in Mephistophelian humor. He can sleep cat-fashion, for sixty seconds at a time, with all his wits about him in the intervals, and likes to feel in the crook of his own forefinger the hidden hair-trigger of events. I don't think Jeremy was awake when I first entered the room, although it suited Grim's humor that he should be presently; but you would have sworn they were both unconscious, judging by the see-saw, bass and baritone snoring.

I poured out whisky, drank a little of it grouchily, and watched Yussuf Dakmar into bed. He didn't take many of his clothes off and even by candle-light you could see the shape of the knife concealed under his shirt. He sat cross-legged on the bed, presumably praying, and as I didn't like the look of him I blew out the candle.

Instantly, pinched and prompted by James Schuyler Grim, Jeremy sat up and yammered profanely at the darkness, vowing he couldn't see to sleep without a light in the room. I tinkled a tumbler against a whisky bottle, and Jeremy instantly swore that he heard burglars. Sitting up and whirling his pillow he knocked Yussuf Dakmar off the bed on to the floor.

So I lit the candle again, after emptying my glass of whisky into a spittoon; whereat Jeremy quoted the Koran about the fate of drunkards and, getting out of bed, apologized to Yussuf Dakmar like a courtier doing homage to a king.

"Your honor was born under a lucky star," he assured him. "I usually shoot or stab, but the pillow was the first thing handy."

The Syrian had hard work to keep his temper, for he had fallen on the haft of the hidden knife and it hurt him between two ribs, where a poorly conditioned man is extra sensitive. However, he mumbled something and crawled between the sheets.

Then Grim vowed that he couldn't sleep with a light so I blew out the candle, and in about two minutes the steady seesaw snoring resumed. I took the opportunity to empty half the contents of a whisky bottle into the spittoon, and after lighting a pipe proceeded to clink a tumbler at steady intervals as evidence of debauch well under way.

Except for the clink and bump of the tumbler, and once when I filled and relit the pipe, all was quiet for half an hour, when Yussuf Dakmar piped up suddenly and asked me whether I didn't intend to come to bed.

"I will not trouble you, effendi. I will keep over to my side. There is plenty of room in the bed for the two of us."

As he spoke I heard a movement of the bedclothes as Grim pinched Jeremy awake again. I answered before Jeremy could horn in.

"Hic! You 'spect me 'nto bed full o' snakes? Never sleep 'slong as venomous reptiles waiting! Hic! You stay 'n bed an keep 'em 'way from me!"

Well, Jeremy didn't want any better cue than that. He got up, lit the candle and explained to me with great wealth of Arabic theosophy that the snakes I saw were mere delusions because Allah never made them; and I tried to look utterly drunk, staring at him with dropped jaw and droopy eyelids, knocking an empty bottle over with my elbow by way of calling attention to it.

"Get into bed, effendi," Jeremy advised me, feeding the cue back, since I was in the middle of the stage.

"Not into that bed!" I answered, shaking my head solemnly. "That f'ler put snakes in on purpose. Why's he sober when I'm drunk? I won't sleep in bed with sober man. Let him get drun' too, an' both see snakes. Then I'll sleep with him!"

Jeremy's roving eye fell on the small doped bottle that I had taken from Grim's valise. Looking preternaturally wise, he walked over to Yussuf Dakmar's bed, sat down on it with his back toward me and proceeded to unfold a plan.

"Allah makes all things easy," he began. "It is lawful to take all precautions to confound the infidel. We shall never get that drunkard to bed as long as there's any whisky, so let's encourage him to drink it all. When it's gone he'll sleep on the floor and we'll get some peace. It's a good chance for us to drink whisky without committing sin! We needn't take much--just one drink each, and then he'll swallow the rest like a hog to prevent our getting any more. You look as if a glass of whisky would do you good. That fellow Omar is asleep and won't see us, so nobody can tell tales afterwards. It's a good opportunity. Come on!"

I had sat so that Yussuf Dakmar couldn't see what I was doing and poured out the liquor in advance, arranging the glasses so that Yussuf Dakmar would take the doped stuff--a perfectly un-Christian proceeding, I admit. Christians are scarce when you get right down to cases. Most of us in extremity prefer Shakespeare's adage about hoisting engineers. It gets results so much more quickly than turning the other cheek. At any rate, I own up.

Yussuf Dakmar, smirking in anticipation of an easy victory, took the nearest tumbler and tossed off the contents in imitation of Jeremy's free and easy air; and the drug acted as swiftly as the famous "knock- out-drops" they used to administer in the New York Tenderloin.

He knew what had happened before he lost consciousness, for he tried to give the alarm to his friends. He lay on the floor opening and shutting his mouth, and I think he believed he was shouting for help; but after a minute or two you could hardly detect his breathing, and his face changed colour as if he had been poisoned.

Grim didn't even trouble to get out of bed, but listened without comment to my version of Narayan Singh's report, and Jeremy went back to sleep chuckling; so I held a silent wake over Yussuf Dakmar, keeping some more of the doped whisky ready in case he should look like recovering too soon. I even searched him, finding nothing worthy of note, except that he had remarkably little money. I expect the poor devil was a penny ante villain scheming for a thousand-dollar jackpot. I felt really sorry for him and turned him over with my boot to let him breathe better.

A little before dawn I awakened Grim and Jeremy and we left the room quietly after I had scratched on the closet door with my fingernails. Pausing outside to listen, we heard the closet door being opened stealthily from the far side. I caught Grim's eye, thinking he would smile back, but he looked as deadly serious as I have ever seen him.

"You made a bad break that time," he said when we had gone downstairs. "Never give away information unless you're getting a return for it! If you'd left Yussuf Dakmar to scratch that door after he recovered consciousness, he'd have invented a pack of lies to tell his friends, and they'd have been no wiser than before. Now they'll know he never scratched it. They'll deduce, unless they're lunatics, that someone overheard their conference last night and knew the signal. That'll make them desperate. They'll waste no more time on finesse. They'll use violence at the first chance after the train leaves Haifa."

"Rammy's like me; he hates not to have an audience for his tricks," put in Jeremy by way of consolation.

"We've got to stage a new play, that's all," said Grim. "I'd have the lot of them arrested, but all the good that would do would be to inform the man higher up, who'd tip off another gang by wire to wait for us over the border. Say, suppose we all three bear this in mind: No play to the gallery! That's where secret service differs from other business. Applause means failure. The better the work you do, the less you can afford to admit you did it. You mustn't even smile at a man you've scored off. Half the game is to leave him guessing who it was that tripped him up. The safest course is to see that someone else gets credit for everything you do."

"Consume your own smoke, eh?" suggested Jeremy.

"That and more," Grim answered. "You've got to work like Bell for what'll do you no good, because the moment it brings you recognition it destroys your usefulness. You mayn't even amuse yourself; you have to let the game amuse you, without turning one trick for the sake of an extra smile; most of the humor comes in anyhow, from knowing more than the other fellow thinks you do. The more a man lies the less you want to contradict him, because if you do he'll know that you know he's lying and that's giving away information, which is the unforgivable sin."

"Golly!" exclaimed Jeremy. "Your trade wouldn't suit me, Jim! When doing tricks, it's good to watch folks' eyes pop open. What tickles my wish-bone is what I can see for myself on their silly faces, half of 'em trying to look as if they know how it's done and the other half all grins. I did tricks for a Scotchman once, who got so angry I thought he'd hit me; he said, what I did was impossible, so I did it again and he still said it was impossible, and he ended by calling me a 'puir dementit men.' That was my apogee; I've never reached that height since, not even when I first made a camel say prayers at Abu Keen and the Arabs hailed me as a prophet! Bread's good, but it's better with the butter on it right side up!"

"Not in this game, it isn't," answered Grim. "If your bread seems smeared with butter that's a sure sign it's dangerous. For God's sake, as long as you stay in the game with me don't play to the gallery, either of you! Let's order breakfast."

It was the longest lecture and expression of opinion I had ever listened to from James Schuyler Grim, and though I've turned it over in my mind a great deal since, I can't discover anything but wisdom in it. I believe he told Jeremy and me the secret of power that morning.

# CHAPTER XI

"They are all right!"

There was no competition for seats on the Damascus train that morning. Several of the window-panes were smashed, there were bullet-marks and splinters on the woodwork everywhere--no need to ask questions. But I found time on the platform to chat with some British officers while keeping an eye lifting for Yussuf Dakmar and his friends.

"Damascus, eh? You'll have a fine journey if you get through alive. Nine passengers were shot dead in the last train down."

"No law up there, you know. Feisul's army's all concentrated for a crack at the French (good luck to 'em! No, I'm not wishing the French any particular luck this trip). Nobody to watch the Bedouins, so they take pot shots at every train that passes, just for the fun of it."

"May be war, you know, at any minute. The French are sure to make a drive for the railway line--you'll be hung up indefinitely--commandeered for an ambulance train--shot for the sake of argument--anything at all, in fact. They say those Algerian troops are getting out of hand--paid in depreciated francs and up against the high cost of debauchery. You're taking a chance."

"Wish I could go. Haven't seen a healthy scrap sinze Zeitun Ridge. Hey! Hullo! What's this? Lovely woman! Well, I'll be!"

It was Mabel Ticknor, followed by the six men I was watching for, Yussuf Dakmar looking sulky and discouraged in their midst, almost like a prisoner, and the other five wearing palpably innocent expressions.

"Lord!" remarked the officer nearest me. "That gang's got the wind up! Look at the color of their gills! Booked through, I'll bet you, and been listening to tales all night!"

The gang drew abreast just as another officer gave tongue to his opinion. They couldn't help hearing what he said; he had one of those voices that can carry on conversation in a boiler foundry.

"There's more in this than meets the eye! She's not a nurse. She don't walk like a missionary. I heard her buy a ticket for Aleppo. Can you imagine a lone, good-looking woman going to Aleppo by that train unless she had a laissez passe from the French? She's wearing French heels. I'll bet she's carrying secret information. Look! D'you see those two Arabs in the train?" He pointed out Grim and Jeremy, who were leaning from a window. "They tipped her off to get into the compartment next ahead of them. D'you see? There she goes. She was for getting into the coach ahead. They called her back."

Almost all the other cars were empty except that one, but, whether because humans are like sheep and herd together instinctively when afraid, or because the train crew ordered it, all six compartments of the middle first-class car were now occupied, with Mabel Ticknor alone in the front one. Nevertheless, Yussuf Dakmar and four of his companions started to climb in by the rear door. The sixth man lingered within earshot of the officers, presumably to pick up further suggestions.

So I got in at the front end and met them halfway down the corridor.

"Plenty of room in the car behind," I said abruptly.

They were five to one, but Yussuf Dakmar was in front, and he merely got in the way of the wolves behind him. The sixth man, who had lingered near the officers, now entered by the front end as I had done and called out that there was plenty of room in the front compartment.

"There's only a woman in here," he said in Arabic.

And he set the example by taking the seat opposite to Mabel.

It would have been easy enough to get him out again, of course. Not even the polyglot train crew would have allowed Arabs to trespass without her invitation.

The trouble was that Jeremy, Grim, Narayan Singh and I all rushed to her rescue at the same minute, which let the cat out of the bag. It was Doctor Ticknor's statement in Jerusalem about not wanting to see any of us alive again if we failed to bring his wife back safe that turned the trick and caused even Grim to lose his head for a moment. When a Sikh, two obvious Arabs and an American all rush to a woman's assistance before she calls for help, there is evidence of collusion somewhere which you could hardly expect a trained spy to overlook or fail to draw conclusions from.

It was all over in a minute. The rascal left the compartment, muttering to himself in Arabic sotto voce. I caught one word; but he looked so diabolically pleased with himself that it didn't really need that to stir me into action. I take twelves in boots, with a rather broad toe, and he stopped the full heft of the hardest kick I could let loose. It put him out of action for half a day, and remains one of my pleasantest memories.

His companions had to gather him up and help him pulley-hauley fashion into the car ahead, while an officious ticket-taker demanded my name and address. I found in my wallet the card of a U.S. senator and gave him that, whereat he apologized profoundly and addressed me as "Colonel"--a title with which he continued to flatter me all the rest of the journey except once, when he changed it to "Admiral" by mistake.

Grim went back into our compartment and laughed; and none of the essays I have read on laughter--not even the famous dissertation by Josh Billings--throw light on how to describe the tantalizing manner of it. He laughs several different ways: heartily at times, as men of my temperament mostly do; boisterously on occasion, after Jeremy's fashion; now and then cryptically, using laughter as a mask; then he owns a smile that suggests nothing more nor less than kindness based on understanding of human nature.

But that other is a devil of a laugh, mostly made of chuckles that seem to bubble off a Bell-brew of disillusionment, and you get the impression that he is laughing at himself--cynically laying bare the vanity and fallibility of his own mental processes--and forecasting self-discipline.

There is no mirth in it, although there is amusement; no anger, although immeasurable scorn. I should say it's a good safe laugh to indulge in, for I think it is based on ability to see himself and his own mistakes more clearly than anybody else can, and there is no note of defeat in it. But it is full of a cruel irony that brings to mind a vision of one of those old medieval flagellant priests reviewing his sins before thrashing his own body with a wire whip.

"So that ends that," he said at last, with the gesture of a man who sweeps the pieces from a board, to set them up anew and start again. "Luckily we're not the only fools in Asia. Those six rascals know now that Mabel and we are one party."

"Pooh!" sneered Jeremy. "What can the devils do?"

"Not much this side of the border at Deraa," Grim answered. "After Deraa pretty well what they're minded. They could have us pinched on some trumped-up charge, in which case we'd be searched, Mabel included. No. We've played too long on the defensive. Deraa is the danger-point. The telegraph line is cut there, and all messages going north or south have to be carried by hand across the border. The French have an agent there who censors everything. He's the boy we've got to fool. If they appeal to him this train will go on without us.

"Ramsden, you and Narayan Singh go and sit with Mabel in her compartment. Jeremy, you go forward and bring Yussuf Dakmar back here to me; we'll let him have that fake letter just before we reach Deraa, taking care somehow to let the other five know he has it. They won't discover it's a fake until after leaving Deraa--"

"Why not?" I interrupted. "What's to prevent their opening it at once?"

"Two good reasons: for one, we'll have Narayan Singh keep a careful eye on them, and they'll keep it hidden as long as he snoops around; for another, they'll be delighted not to have to let the French agent at Deraa into the secret, because of the higher price they hope to get by holding on. They'll smuggle it over the border and not open it until they feel safe."

"Yes, but when they do look at it ..." said I.

"We'll be over the border, and they can't send telegrams to anywhere."

"Why not?"

"An Arab government precaution. If station agents all along the line were allowed to send telegrams every seditious upstart would take advantage of it and they'd have more trouble than they've got now. But I warn you fellows, after Deraa--somewhere between the border and Damascus--there'll be a fight. The minute they discover that the letter is a fake they'll come for the real one like cats after a canary."

"Let 'em come!" smiled Jeremy, but Grim shook his head. "I've been making that mistake too long," he answered. "No defensive tactics after we leave Deraa! We'll start the trouble ourselves. You watch, after Deraa the train crew will play cards in the caboose and leave Allah to care for the passengers."

"There's only one thing troubles me," said Jeremy.

"What's that?"

"Narayan Singh got Yussuf Dakmar's shirt night before last. I've had it in for Yussuf ever since we Anzacs went hungry on account of him. Anyone who scuppers him has got me to beat to him. He's my meat, and I give you all notice!"

It isn't good to stand between an Anzac and the punishment he thinks an enemy deserves.

"All the same," Grim answered, smiling, "I'll bet you don't get him, Jeremy."

"I'll bet you. How much?"

"Mind you, when the game begins, you have a free hand," Grim went on.

"All right," answered Jeremy, who loves freak bets, ''if I get him you quit the Army soon as this job's done, and join up with Rammy and me: if I don't I'll stay and help you on the next job."

"That's a bet," said Grim promptly.

So Jeremy went forward to play at being traitor, while Narayan Singh and I kept Mabel company. She fired questions at us right and left for twenty minutes, which we had to answer in detail instead of straining our cars to catch what Grim and Jeremy might be saying to Yussuf Dakmar in the next compartment.

Whatever they did say, they managed to prolong the interview until within ten minutes of Deraa, when the Syrian returned to his companions smiling smugly and Narayan Singh strode after him, to stand in the corridor and by ostentatiously watching them prevent their examining the letter.

Grim and Jeremy, all grins, joined us at once in Mabel's compartment.

"Did you see the devil smirk as he went off with it?" asked Jeremy. "Golly, he thinks we're fools! The theory is that we two had betrayed you, Rammy, and swapped the letter against his bare promise to pay us in Damascus. He chucked in a little blackmail about sicking his mates on to murder us if we didn't come across, and I tell you we fairly love him! Lordy, here's Deraa! If they open the thing before the train leaves, Grim says the lot of us are to bolt back across the border, send Mabel home to her husband, and continue the journey by camel. That right, Grim?"

Grim nodded. It was Mabel who objected.

"I'm going to see this through," she answered. "Guess again, boys! My hair's gone gray. You owe me a real adventure now, and I won't give up the letter till you've paid!"

We had one first-class scare when the train drew up in the squalid station, where the branch line to Haifa meets the main Hedjaz railway and the two together touch a mean town at a tangent; for a French officer in uniform boarded the train and stalked down the corridors staring hard at everyone. He asked me for a passport, which was sheer bluff, so I asked him in turn for his own authority. He smiled and produced a rubber stamp, saying that if I wished to visit Beirut or Aleppo I must get a vise from him.

"Je m'em been garderai!" I answered. "I'm going to see my aunt at Damascus."

"And this lady? Is she your wife?"

I laughed aloud--couldn't help it. All the Old Testament stories keep forcing themselves on your memory in that land, and the legend of Abraham trying to pass his wife off as his sister and the three-cornered drama that came of it cropped up as fresh as yesterday. There was no need that I could see to repeat the patriarch's mistake, any more than there was reasonable basis for the Frenchman's impertinence.

"Is that your business?" I asked him.

"Because," he went on, smiling meanly, "you speak with an American accent. It is against the law to carry gold across the border, and Americans have to submit to personal search, because they always carry it."

"Show me your authority!" I retorted angrily.

"Oh, as for that, there is a customs official here who has full authority. He is a Syrian. It occurred to me that you might prefer to be searched by a European."

"Call his bluff!" Grim whispered behind his sleeve, but I intended to do that, anyway.

"Bring along your Syrian," said I, and off he went to do it, treating me to a backward glance over his shoulder that conveyed more than words could have done.

"He'll bluff sky-high," said Grim, "but keep on calling him."

"I've been searched at six frontiers," said Mabel. "If it's a Syrian I don't much mind; you boys all come along, and he'll behave himself. They're much worse in France and Italy. Hadn't one of you better take the letter, though? No! I was forgetting already! I won't part with it. I'll take my chance with the Syrian; he'll only ask me to empty my pockets and prove that I haven't a bag full of gold under my skirt. Sit tight, all, here he comes!"

The Frenchman returned with a smiling, olive-complexioned Syrian in tow --a round-faced fellow with blue jaws as dark as his serge uniform. The Frenchman stood aside and the Syrian announced rather awkwardly that regulations compelled him to submit Mabel and me to the inconvenience of search.

"For what?" said I.

"For gold," he answered. "It is against the law to smuggle it across the border."

"I've only one gold coin," I said, showing him a U.S. twenty-dollar piece, and his yellow eyes shone at sight of it. "If it will save trouble you may have it."

I put it into his open palm with the Frenchman looking on, and it was immediately clear that that particular Syrian official was no longer amenable to international intrigue. He was bought and sold--oozy with gratitude--incapable of anything but wild enthusiasm for the U.S.A. for several hours to come.

"I have searched them!" said he to the French officer. "They have no gold, and they are all right."

The French have faults like the rest of us, but they are quicker than most men to recognize logic. The man with crimson pants and sabre grinned cynically, shrugged his shoulders, and passed on to annoy somebody easier.

---

# CHAPTER XII

"Start something before they're ready for it!"

Just before the train started, a handsome fellow with short black beard trimmed into a point and wearing a well-cut European blue serge suit, but none the less obviously an Arab, came to the door of our compartment and stared steadily at Grim. He stood like a fighting man, as if every muscle of his body was under command, and the suggestion was strengthened by what might be a bullet scar over one eye.

If that fellow had asked me for a loan on the spot, or for help against his enemies, he would have received both or either. Moreover, if he had never paid me back I would still believe in him, and would bet on him again.

However, after one swift glance at him, Grim took no notice until the train was under way--not even then in fact, until the man in blue serge spoke first.

"Oh, Jimgrim!" he said suddenly in a voice like a tenor bell.

"Come in, Hadad," Grim answered, hardly glancing at him. "Make yourself at home."

He tossed a valise into the rack, and I gave up the corner seat so that he might sit facing Grim, he acknowledging the courtesy with a smile like the whicker of a sword-blade, wasting no time on foolish protest. He knew what he wanted--knew enough to take it when invited--understood me, and expected me to understand him--a first-class fellow. He sat leaning a little forward, his back not touching the cushion, with the palms of both hands resting on his knees and strong fingers motionless. He eyed Mabel Ticknor, not exactly nervously but with caution.

"Any news?" asked Grim.

"Jimgrim, the world is full of it!" he answered in English with a laugh. "But who are these?"

"My friends."

"Your intimate friends?" Grim nodded.

"The lady as well?" Grim nodded again.

"That is very strong recommendation, Jimgrim!"

Grim introduced us, giving Jeremy's name as Jmil Ras.

"Hah! I have heard of you," said Hadad, staring at him. "The Australian who wandered all over Arabia? I am probably the only Arab who knew what you really were. Do you recall that time at Wady Hafiz when a local priest denounced you and a Sheik in a yellow kuffiyi told the crowd that he knew you for a prophet? I am the same Sheik. I liked your pluck. I often wondered what became of you."

"Put it here!" said Jeremy, and they shook hands.

For twenty minutes after that Hadad and Jeremy swapped reminiscences in quick staccato time. It was like two Gatling guns playing a duet, and the score was about equally intelligible to anyone unfamiliar with Arabia's hinterland--which is to say to all except about one person in ten million. It was most of it Greek to me, but Grim listened like an operator to the ticking of the Morse code. It was Hadad who cut it short; Jeremy would have talked all the way to Damascus.

"And so, Jimgrim, do the kites foregather? Or are we a forlorn hope? Do we go to bury Feisul or to crown him king?"

"How much do you know?" Grim answered.

"Hah! More than you, my friend! I come from Europe--London--Paris-- Rome. I stopped off in Deraa to listen a while, where the tide of rumour flows back and forth across the border. The English are in favour of Feisul, and would help him if they could. The French are against him and would rather have him a dead saint than a living nuisance. The most disturbing rumour I have heard was here in Deraa, to the effect that Feisul sent a letter to Jerusalem calling on all Moslems to rise and massacre the Jews. That does not sound like Feisul, but the French agent in Deraa assured me that he will have the original letter in his hands within a day or two."

Grim smiled over at Mabel.

"You might show him the letter?" he suggested.

So Mabel dug down into the mysteries beneath her shirtwaist and produced the document wrapped in a medical bandage of oiled silk. Hadad unwrapped it, read it carefully, and handed it to Grim.

"Are you deceived by that?" he asked. "Does Feisul speak like that, or write like that? Since when has he turned coward that he should sign his name with a number?"

"What do you make of it?" asked Grim.

"Hah! It is as plain as the ink on the paper. It is intended for use against Feisul, first by making the British suspicious of him, second by providing the French with an excuse to attack him, third by convicting him of treachery, for which he can be jailed or executed after he is caught. What do you propose to do with it, Jimgrim?"

"I'm going to show it to Feisul."

"Good! I, too, am on my way to see Feisul. Perhaps the two of us together can convince him what is best."

"If we two first agree," Grim answered with a dry smile.

"Do you agree that two and two make four? This is just as simple, Jimgrim. Feisul cannot contend with the French. The financiers have spread their net for Syria, Feisul has no artillery worth speaking of-- no gas--no masks against gas, and the French have plenty of everything except money. Syria has been undermined by propaganda and corruption. Let Feisul go to British territory and thence to Europe, where his friends may have a chance to work for him. The British will give him Mesopotamia, and after that it will be up to us Arabs to prove we are a nation. That is my argument. Are we agreed?"

"If that's your plan, Hadad, I'm with you!" Grim answered.

"Then I also am with you! Let us shake hands."

"Shwai shwai!" (Go slow!) said Grim. "Better join up with me in Damascus. There are six men in the car ahead who'll try to murder us all presently. They've got a letter that they think is that one. The minute they find out we've fooled them there'll be ructions."

"I am good at ructions!" Hadad answered.

"My friend Narayan Singh is forward watching them," said Grim. "What they'll probably try when they make the discovery will be to have the lot of us arrested at some wayside station. I propose to forestall them."

"I am good at forestalling!" said Hadad.

"Then don't you forestall me!" laughed Jeremy. "The fellow with a face like a pig's stern is Yussuf Dakmar, and he's my special preserve."

"I am a good Moslem. I refuse to lay hand on pig," said Hadad, smiling.

We discussed Feisul and the Arab cause.

"Oh, if we had Lawrence with us!" exclaimed Hadad excitedly at last. "A little, little man--hardly any larger than Mrs. Ticknor--but a David against Goliath! And would you believe it?--there is an idiotic rumour that Lawrence has returned and is hiding in Damascus! The French are really disturbed about it. They have cabled their Foreign Office and received an official denial of the rumour; but official denials carry no weight nowadays. Out of ten Frenchmen in Syria, five believe that Lawrence is with Feisul and if they can catch him he will get short shrift. But, oh, Jimgrim--oh, if it were true! Wallahi!"

Grim didn't answer, but I saw him look long at Jeremy, and then for about thirty seconds steadily at Mabel Ticknor. After that he stared out of the window for a long time, not even moving his head when a crowd of Bedouins galloped to within fifty yards of the train and volleyed at it from horseback "merely out of devilment," as Hadad hastened to assure us.

We were winding up the Lebanon Valley by that time. Carpets of flowers; green grass; waterfalls; a thatched hut to the twenty square miles, with a scattering of mean black tents between; every stone building in ruins; goats where fat kine ought to be; and a more or less modern railway screeching across the landscape, short of fuel and oil. That's Lebanon.

We grew depressed. Then silent. Our meditations were interrupted by the sudden arrival of Narayan Singh in the door of the compartment, grinning full of news.

"They have opened the letter, sahib! They accuse Yussuf Dakmar of deceiving them. They threaten him with death. Shall I interfere?"

"Any sign of the train crew?" Grim asked.

"Nay, they are gambling in the brake-van."

Grim looked sharply at Hadad.

"What authority have you got?"

"None. I am a personal friend of Feisul, that is all."

"Well, we'll pretend you've power to arrest them. Ramsden, you've suddenly missed your letter. You've accused Jeremy of stealing it. He has confessed to selling it to Yussuf Dakmar. Go forward in a rage and demand the letter back. Start something before they're ready for it! We'll be just behind you."

"Leave Yussuf Dakmar to me!" insisted Jeremy. "I pay the debt of an Anzac division!"

I hope I've never hurt a man who didn't deserve it, or who wasn't fit to fight; but I have to admit that Grim didn't need to repeat the invitation. I started forward in a hurry, and Jeremy elbowed Narayan Singh aside in order to follow next, Australians being notoriously unlady-like performers when anybody's hat is in the ring.

By the time I reached the car ahead the train had entered a wild gorge circle by one of those astonishing hairpin curves with which engineers defeat Nature. The panting engine slowed almost to a snail's pace, having only a scant fuel ration with which to negotiate curve and grade combined. To our right there was a nearly sheer drop of four hundred feet, with a stream at the bottom boiling among limestone boulders.

But there was no time to study scenery. From the middle compartment of the car there came yells for help and the peculiar noise of thump and scuffle that can't be mistaken. Men fight in various ways, Lord knows, and the worst are the said-to-be civilized; but from Nome to Cape Town and all the way from China to Peru the veriest tenderfoot can tell in the dark the difference between fight and horseplay.

I reached the door of the compartment in time to see three of them (two bleeding from knife-wounds in the face) force Yussuf Dakmar backward toward the window, the whole lot stabbing frantically as they milled and swayed. The fifth man was holding on to the scrimmage with his left hand and reaching round with his right, trying to stick a knife into Yussuf Dakmar's ribs without endangering his own hide.

But the sixth man was the rascal I had kicked. He had no room--perhaps no inclination--to get into the scrimmage; so he saw me first, and he needed no spur to his enmity. With a movement as quick as a cat's and presence of mind that accounted for his being leader of the gang, he seized the fifth man by the neck and spun him round to call his attention; and the two came for me together like devils out of a spring-trap.

Now the narrow door of a compartment on a train isn't any kind of easy place to fight in, but I vow and declare that Jeremy and I both did our best for Yussuf Dakmar. That's a remarkable thing if you come to think of it. As a dirty murderer--thief--liar--traitor--spy, he hadn't much claim on our affections and Jeremy cherished a war-grudge against him on top of it all. What is it that makes us side with the bottom dog regardless of pros and cons?

It was a nasty mix-up, because they used knives and we relied on hands and fists. I've used a pick-handle on occasion and a gun when I've had to, but speaking generally it seems to me to demean a white man to use weapons in a row like that, and I find that most fellows who have walked the earth much agree with me.

We tried to go in like a typhoon, shock-troop style, but it didn't work. Another man let go of Yussuf Dakmar, who was growing weak and too short of wind to yell, and in a moment there were five of us struggling on the floor between the seats, one man under me with my forearm across his throat and another alongside me, stabbing savagely at a leather valise under the impression that he was carving up my ribs. On top of that mess Narayan Singh pounced like a tiger, wrenching at arms and legs until I struggled to my feet again--only to be thrust aside by Jeremy as he rose and rushed at Yussuf Dakmar's two assailants.

But with all his speed Jeremy was a tenth of a tick too late. The wretch was already helpless, and I dare say they broke his back as they leaned their combined weight on him and forced him backward and head-first through the window. Jeremy made a grab for his foot, but missed it, and a knife-blade already wet with Yussuf Dakmar's blood whipped out and stung him in the thigh. That, of course, was sheer ignorance. You should never sting an Australian. Kill him or let him alone. Better yet, make friends with him or surrender; but, above all, do nothing by halves. They're a race of whole-hoggers, equally ready to force their only shirt on you or fight you to a finish.

So Jeremy finished the business at the window. He took a neck in each hand and cracked their skulls together until the whack-whack-whack of it was like the exhaust of a Ford with loose piston rings; and when they fell from his grip, unconscious, he came to my rescue. Believe me, I needed it.

They were as strong and lithe as wildcats, those Syrians, and fully awake to the advantage that the narrow door gave them. One man struggled with Narayan Singh and kept him busy with his bulk so wedged across the opening that Grim and Ha-dad were as good as demobilized out in the corridor; and the other two tackled me like a pair of butchers hacking at a maddened bull. I landed with my fists, but each time at the cost of a flesh-wound; and though I got one knife-hand by the wrist and hung on, wrenching and screwing to throw the fellow off his feet, the other man's right was free and the eighteen-inch Erzeram dagger that he held danced this and that way for an opening underneath my guard.

Jeremy's left fist landed under the peak of his jaw exactly at the moment when he stiffened to launch his thrust. He fell as if pole-axed and the blade missed my stomach by six inches, but the combined force of thrust and blow was great enough to drive the weapon into the wooden partition, where it stayed until I pulled it out to keep as a souvenir.

There wasn't much trouble after that. Grim and Hadad came in and we tore strips from the Syrians' clothing to tie their hands and feet with. Hadad went to the rear of the train, climbing along the footboard of the third-class cars to the caboose to throw some sort of bluff to the conductor, who came forward--called me "Colonel" and Hadad "Excellency" --looked our prisoners over--recognized no friends--and said that everything was "quite all right." He said he knew exactly what to do; but we left Narayan Singh on watch, lest that knowledge should prove too original which, however, it turned out not to be. It was bromidian--as old as history. Narayan Singh came back and told us.

"Lo, sahib; he went through their clothes as an ape for fleas, I watching. And when he had all their valuables he laid them on the footboard, and then, as we passed some Bedouin tents, he kicked them off. But he seems an honest fellow, for he gave them back some small change to buy food with, should any be obtain-able."

After that he stood flashing his white teeth for half an hour watching Mabel bandage Jeremy and me, for it always amuses a Sikh to watch a white man eat punishment. Sikhs are a fine race--but curious-- distinctly curious and given to unusual amusement. When Mabel had finished with me at last I stuck a needle into him, and he laughed, accepting the stab as a compliment.

A strange thing is how men settle down after excitement. Birds do the same thing. A hawk swoops down on a hedgerow; there is a great flutter, followed by sudden silence. A minute later the chattering begins again, without any reference to one of their number being torn in the plunderer's beak. And so we; even Grim loosened up and gossiped about Feisul and the already ancient days when Feisul was the up-to-date Saladin leading Arab hosts to victory.

But there was an even stranger circumstance than that. We weren't the only people in the train; our car, for instance, was fairly well occupied by Armenians, Arabs, and folk whose vague nationality came under the general heading of Levantine. The car ahead where the fight took place, though not crowded, wasn't vacant, and there were others in the car behind. Yet not one of them made a move to interfere. They minded their own business, which proves, I think, that manners are based mainly on discretion.

As the train gasped slowly up the grade and rolled bumpily at last along the fertile, neglected Syrian highland, all the Armenians on the train removed their hats and substituted the red tarboosh, preferring the headgear of a convert rather than be the target of every Bedouin with a rifle in his hand.

The whole journey was a mix-up of things to wonder at--not least of them the matter-of-fact confidence with which the train proceeded along a single track, whose condition left you wondering at each bump whether the next wouldn't be the journey's violent end. There were lamps, but no oil for light when evening came. Once, when we bumped over a shaky culvert and a bushel or two of coal-dust fell from the rusty tender, the engineer stopped the train and his assistant went back with a shovel and piece of sacking to gather up the precious stuff.

There was nothing but squalid villages and ruins, goats and an occasional rare camel to be seen through the window--not a tree anywhere, the German General Staff having attended to that job thoroughly. There is honey in the country and it's plentiful as well as good, because bees are not easy property to raid and make away with; but the milk is from goats, and as for overflowing, I would hate to have to punish the dugs of a score of the brutes to get a jugful for dinner. Syria's wealth is of the past and the future.

Long before it grew too dark to watch the landscape we were wholly converted to Grim's argument that Syria was no place for a man of Feisul's calibre. The Arab owners of the land are plundered to the bone; the men with money are foreigners, whose only care is for a government that will favour this religion and that breed.

To set up a kingdom there would be like preaching a new religion in Hester Street; you could hand out text, soup and blankets, but you'd need a whale's supply of faith to carry on, and the offertories wouldn't begin to meet expenses.

Until that journey finally convinced me, I had been wondering all the while in the back of my head whether Grim wasn't intending an impertinence. It hasn't been my province hitherto to give advice to kings; for one thing, they haven't asked me for it. If I were asked, I think I'd take the problem pretty seriously and hesitate before suggesting to a man on whom the hope of fifty million people rests that he'd better pull up stakes and eat crow in exile for the present. I'd naturally hate to be a king, but if I were one I don't think quitting would look good, and I think I'd feel like kicking the fellow who suggested it.

But the view from the train, and Grim's talk with Hadad put me in a mood in which Syria didn't seem good enough for a soap-box politician, let alone a man of Feisul's fame and character. And when at last a few lights in a cluster down the track proclaimed that we were drawing near Damascus, I was ready to advise everybody, Feisul included, to get out in a hurry while a chance remained.

## CHAPTER XIII

"Bismillah!  What a mercy that I met you!"

W hile the fireman scraped the iron floor for his last two shovelfuls of coal-dust and the train wheezed wearily into the dark station, Grim began to busy himself in mysterious ways.  Part of his own costume consisted of a short, curved scimitar attached to an embroidered belt-- the sort of thing that Arabs wear for ornament rather than use.  He took it off and, groping in the dark, helped Mabel put it on, without a word of explanation.

Then, instead of putting on his own Moslem over-cloak he threw that over her shoulders and, digging down into his bag for a spare head-dress, snatched her hat off and bound on the white kerchief in its place with the usual double, gold-covered cord of camel-hair.

Then came my friend the train conductor and addressed me as Colonel, offering to carry out the bags.  The moment he had grabbed his load and gone Grim broke silence:

"Call her Colonel and me Grim.  Don't forget how!"

We became aware of faces under helmets peering through the window- officers of Feisul's army on the watch for unwelcome visitors.  From behind them came the conductor's voice again, airing his English:

"Any more bags inside there, Colonel?"

"Get out quick, Jeremy, and make a fuss about the Colonel coming!" ordered Grim.

Jeremy suddenly became the arch-efficient servitor, establishing importance for his chief, and never a newly made millionaire or modern demagog had such skillful advertisement.  The Shereefian officers stood back at a respectful distance, ready to salute when the personage should deign to alight.

"What shall be done with the memsahib's hat?" demanded Narayan Singh.

You could only see the whites of his eyes, but he shook something in his right hand.

"Eat it!" Grim answered.

"Heavens! That's my best hat!" objected Mabel. "Give it here. I'll carry it under the cloak."

"Get rid of it!" Grim ordered; and Narayan Singh strode off to contribute yellow Leghorn straw and poppies to the engine furnace.

I gave him ten piastres to fee the engineer, and five for the fireman, so you might say that was high-priced fuel.

"What kind of bunk are you throwing this time?" I asked Grim.

He didn't answer, but gave orders to Mabel in short, crisp syllables.

"You're Colonel Lawrence. Answer no questions. If anyone salutes, just move your hand and bow your head a bit. You're just his height. Look straight in front of you and take long strides. Bend your head forward a little; there, that's it."

"I'm scared!" announced Mabel, by way of asking for more particulars.

She wasn't scared in the least.

"Piffle!" Grim answered. "Remember you're Lawrence, that's all. They'd give you Damascus if you asked for it. Follow Jeremy, and leave the rest to us."

I don't doubt that Grim had been turning over the whole plan in his mind for hours past, but when I taxed him with it afterward his reply was characteristic:

"If we'd rehearsed it, Mabel and Hadad would both have been self-conscious. The game is to study your man--or woman, as the case may be--and sometimes drill 'em, sometimes spring it on 'em, according to circumstances. The only rule is to study people; there are no two quite alike."

Hadad was surprised into silence, too thoughtful a man to do anything except hold his tongue until the next move should throw more light on the situation. He followed us out of the car, saying nothing; and being recognized by the light of one dim lantern as an intimate friend of Feisul, he accomplished all that Grim could have asked of him.

He was known to have been in Europe until recently. Rumours about Lawrence had been tossed from mouth to mouth for days past, and here was somebody who looked like Lawrence in the dark, followed by Grim and Hadad and addressed as "Colonel." Why shouldn't those three Shereefian officers jump to conclusions, salute like automatons and grin like loyal men who have surprised a secret and won't tell anyone but their bosom friends? It was all over Damascus within the hour that Lawrence had come from England to stand by Feisul in the last ditch. The secret was kept perfectly!

We let Mabel walk ahead of us, and there was no trouble at the customs barrier, where normally every piastre that could be wrung from protesting passengers were mulcted to support a starving treasury; for the officers strode behind us, and trade signs to the customs clerk, who immediately swore at everyone in sight and sent all his minions to yell for the best cabs in Damascus.

Narayan Singh distributed largesse to about a hundred touts and hangers-on and we splashed off toward the hotel in two open landaus, through streets six inches deep in water except at the cross-gutters, where the horses jumped for fear of losing soundings. Abana and Pharpar, rivers of Damascus, were in flood as usual at that time of year, and the scavenging street curs had to swim from one garbage heap to the next. There was a gorgeous battle going on opposite the hotel door, where half a dozen white-ivoried mongrels with their backs to a heap of kitchen leavings held a ford against a dozen others, each beast that made good his passage joining with the defenders to fight off the rest. I stood on the hotel steps and watched the war for several minutes, while Grim went in with the others and registered as "Rupert Ramsden of Chicago, U.S.A., and party."

The flood, and darkness owing to the lack of fuel, were all in our favour, for such folk as were abroad were hardly of the sort whose gossip would carry weight; nevertheless, we hadn't been in the hotel twenty minutes before an agent of the bank put in his appearance, speaking French volubly. Seeing my name on the register, he made the mistake of confining his attention to me, which enabled Grim to get Mabel safely away into a big room on the second floor.

The Frenchman (if he was one--he had a Hebrew nose) made bold to corner me on a seat near the dining-room door. He was nervous rather than affable--a little pompous, as behooved the representative of money power--and evidently used to having his impertinences answered humbly.

"You are from the South? Did you have a good journey? Was the train attacked? Did you hear any interesting rumors on the way?"

Those were all preliminary questions, thrown out at random to break ice. As he sat down beside me you could feel the next one coming just as easily as see that he wasn't interested in the answers to the first.

"You are here on business? What business?"

"Private business," said I, with an eye on Jeremy just coming down the stairs. "You talk Arabic?"

He nodded, eyeing me keenly.

"That man is my servant and knows my affairs. I'm too tired to talk after the journey. Suppose you ask him."

So Jeremy came and sat beside us, and threw the cow's husband around as blithely as he juggles billiard balls. I wasn't supposed to understand what he was saying.

"The big effendi is a prizefighter, who has heard there is money to be made at Feisul's court. At least, that is what he says. Between you and me, I think he is a spy for the French Government, because when he engaged me in Jerusalem he gave me a fist-full of paper francs with which to send a telegram to Paris. What was in the telegram? I don't know; it was a mass of figures, and I mixed them up on purpose, being an honest fellow averse to spy's work. Oh, I've kept an eye on him, believe me! Ever since he killed a Syrian in the train I've had my doubts of him. Mashallah, what a murderous disposition the fellow has! Kill a man as soon as look at him-- indeed he would. Are you a prince in these parts?"

"A banker."

"Bismillah! What a mercy that I met you! I overheard him say that he will visit the bank tomorrow morning to cash a draft for fifty thousand francs. I'd examine the draft carefully if I were you. It wouldn't surprise me to learn it was stolen or forged. Is there any other bank that he could go to?"

"No, only mine; the others have suspended business on account of the crisis."

"Then, in the name of Allah don't forget me! You ought to give me a thousand francs for the information. I am a poor man, but honest. At what time shall I come for the money in the morning? Perhaps you could give me a little on account at once, for my wages are due tonight and I'm not at all certain of getting them."

"Well, see me in the morning," said the banker.

He got up and left us at once, hardly troubling to excuse himself; and Grim heard him tell the hotel proprietor that our whole party would be locked up in jail before midnight. That rumour went the rounds like wild-fire, so that we were given a wide berth and had a table all to ourselves in the darkest corner of the big dim dining-room.

There were more than a hundred people eating dinner, and Narayan Singh, Hadad and I were the only ones in western clothes. Every seat at the other tables was occupied by some Syrian dignitary in flowing robes-- rows and rows of stately looking notables, scant of speech and noisy at their food. Many of them seemed hardly to know the use of knife and fork, but they could all look as dignified as owls, even when crowding in spaghetti with their fingers.

We provided them with a sensation before the second course was finished. A fine-looking Syrian officer in khaki, with the usual cloth flap behind his helmet that forms a compromise between western smartness and eastern comfort, strode into the room and bore down on us. He invited us out into the corridor with an air that suggested we would better not refuse, and we filed out after him in an atmosphere of frigid disapproval.

Mabel was honestly scared half out of her wits now. Not even the smiles of the hotel proprietor in the doorway reassured her, nor his deep bow as she passed. She was even more scared, if that were possible, when two officers, obviously of high rank, came forward in the hall to greet her, and one addressed her in Arabic as Colonel Lawrence. Luckily one oil lamp per wall was doing duty in place of electric light, or there might have been an awkward incident. She had presence of mind enough to disguise her alarm by a fit of coughing, bending nearly double and cover-ing the lower part of her face with the ends of the headdress folded over.

The officers had no time to waste and gave their message to Grim instead.

"The Emir Feisul is astonished, Jimgrim, that Colonel Lawrence and you should visit Damascus without claiming his hospitality. We have two autos waiting to take you to the palace."

Well, the luggage didn't amount to much; Narayan Singh brought that down in a jiffy; and when I went to settle with the hotel-keeper one of the Syrian officers interfered.

"These are guests of the Emir Feisul," he announced. "Send the bill to me."

We were piled into the waiting autos. Mabel, Grim and I rode in the first one, with the Syrian officers up beside the driver; Jeremy, Narayan Singh and Hadad followed; and we went through the dark streets like sea-monsters splashing over shoals, unseen I think--certainly unrecognized.

The streets were almost deserted and I didn't catch sight of one armed man, which was a thing to marvel at when you consider that fifty thousand or so were supposed to be concentrated in the neighbourhood, with conscription working full-blast and the foreign consuls solely occupied in procuring exemption for their nationals.

It wasn't my first visit to a reigning prince, for if you travel much in India you're bound to come in contact with numbers of them; so I naturally formed a mental picture of what was in store for us, made up from a mixture of memories of Gwalior, Baroda, Bikanir, Hyderabad, Poona and Baghdad of the Arabian-Nights. It just as naturally vanished in presence of the quiet, latter-day dignity of the real thing.

The palace turned out to be a villa on the outskirts of the city, no bigger and hardly more pretentious than a well-to-do commuter's place at Bronxville or Mount Vernon. There was a short semi-circular drive in front, with one sentry and one small lantern burning at each gate; but their khaki uniforms and puttees didn't disguise the fact that the sentries were dark, dyed-in-wool Arabs from the desert country, and though they presented arms, they did it as men who make concessions without pretending to admire such foolishness. I wouldn't have given ten cents for an unescorted stranger's chance of getting by them, whatever his nationality.

Surely there was never less formality in a king's house since the world began. We were ushered straight into a narrow, rather ordinary hall, and through that into a sitting-room about twenty feet square. The light was from oil lamps hanging by brass chains from the curved beams; but the only other Oriental suggestions were the cushioned seats in each corner, small octagonal tables inlaid with mother-of-pearl, and a mighty good Persian carpet.

Narayan Singh and Jeremy, supposedly being servants, offered to stay in the hall, but were told that Feisul wouldn't approve of that.

"Whatever they shouldn't hear can be said in another room," was the explanation.

So we all sat down together on one of the corner seats, and were kept waiting about sixty seconds until Feisul entered by a door in the far corner. And when he came he took your breath away.

It always prejudices me against a man to be told that he is dignified and stately. Those adjectives smack of too much self-esteem and of a claim to be made of different clay from most of us. He was both, yet he wasn't either. And he didn't look like a priest, although if ever integrity and righteousness shone from a man, with their effect heightened by the severely simple Arab robes, I swear that man was he.

Just about Jeremy's height and build--rather tall and thin that is--with a slight stoop forward from the shoulders due to thoughtfulness and camel-riding and a genuine intention not to hold his head too high, he looked like a shepherd in a Bible picture, only with good humour added, that brought him forward out of a world of dreams on to the same plane with you, face to face--understanding meeting understanding--man to man.

I wish I could describe his smile as he entered, believing he was coming to meet Lawrence, but it can't be done. Maybe you can imagine it if you bear in mind that this man was captain of a cause as good as lost, hedged about by treason and well aware of it; and that Colonel Lawrence was the one man in the world who had proved himself capable of bridging the division between East and West and making possible the Arab dream of independence.

But unhappily it's easier to record unpleasant things. He knew at the first glance--even before she drew back the kuffiyi--that Mabel wasn't Lawrence, and I've never seen a man more disappointed in all my wanderings. The smile didn't vanish; he had too much pluck and self-control for that; but you might say that iron entered into it, as if for a second he was mocking destiny, willing to face all odds alone since he couldn't have his friend.

And he threw off disappointment like a man--dismissed it as a rock sheds water, coming forward briskly to shake hands with Grim and bowing as Grim introduced us.

"At least here are two good friends," he said in Arabic, sitting down between Grim and Hadad. "Tell me what this means, and why you deceived us about Lawrence."

"We've something to show you," Grim answered. "Mrs. Ticknor brought it;

otherwise it might have been seen by the wrong people."

Feisul took the hint and dismissed the Syrian officers, calling them by their first names as he gave them "leave to go." Then Mabel produced the letter and Feisul read it, crossing one thin leg over the other and leaning back easily. But he sat forward again and laughed bitterly when he had read it twice over.

"I didn't write this. I never saw it before, or heard of it," he said simply.

"I know that," said Grim. "But we thought you'd better look at it."

Feisul laid the letter across his knee and paused to light a cigarette. I thought he was going to do what nine men out of ten in a tight place would certainly have done; but he blew out the match, and went on smoking.

"You mean your government has seen the thing, and sent you to confront me with it?"

It was Grim's turn to laugh, and he was jubilant without a trace of bitterness.

"No. The chief and I have risked our jobs by not reporting it. This visit is strictly unofficial."

Feisul handed the letter back to him, and it was Grim who struck a match and burned it, after tearing off the seal for a memento.

"You know what it means, of course?" Grim trod the ash into the carpet. "If the French could have come by that letter in Jerusalem, they'd have Dreyfussed you-- put you on trial for your life on trumped-up evidence. They'd send a sworn copy of it to the British to keep them from taking your part."

"I am grateful to you for burning it," Feisul answered.

He didn't look helpless, hopeless, or bewildered, but dumb and clinging on; like a man who holds an insecure footing against a hurricane.

"It means that the men all about you are traitors--" Grim went on.

"Not all of them," Feisul interrupted.

"But many of them," answered Grim. "Your Arabs are loyal hot-heads; some of your Syrians are dogs whom anyone can hire."

It was straight speaking. From a major in foreign service, uninvited, to a king, it sounded near the knuckle. Feisul took it quite pleasantly.

"I know one from the other, Jimgrim."

Grim got up and took a chair opposite Feisul. He was all worked up and sweating at self-mastery, hotter under the collar than I had ever seen him.

"It means," he went on, with a hand on each knee and his strange eyes fixed steadily on Feisul's, "that the French are ready to attack you. It means they're sure of capturing your person--and bent on seeing your finish. They'll give you a drumhead court martial and make excuses afterward."

"Inshallah," Feisul answered, meaning "If Allah permits it."

"That is exactly the right word!" Grim exploded; and Lord, he was hard put to it to keep excitement within bounds.

I could see his neck trembling, and there were little beads of sweat on his temple. It was Grim at last without the mask on. "Allah marks the destiny of all of us. Do you suppose we're here for nothing--at this time?"

Feisul smiled.

"I am glad to see you," he said simply.

"Are you planning to fight the French?" Grim asked him suddenly, in the sort of way that a man at close quarters lets rip an upper-cut.

"I must fight or yield. They have sent an ultimatum, but delayed it so as not to permit me time to answer. It has expired already. They are probably advancing."

"And you intend to sit here and wait for them?"

"I shall be at the front."

"You know you haven't a chance!"

"My advisers think that my presence at the front will encourage our men sufficiently to win the day."

"Have you a charm against mustard gas?"

"That is our weakness. No, we have no masks."

"And the wind setting up from the sea at this time of year! Your army is going straight into a trap, and you along with it. Half of the men who advise you to go to the front will fight like lions against a net, and the other half will sell you to the French! Your fifty thousand men will melt like butter in the sun and your Arab cause will be left without a leader!"

Feisul pondered that for about a minute, leaning back and watching Grim's face.

"We held a council of war, Jimgrim," he said at last. "It was the unanimous opinion of the staff that we ought to fight and the cabinet upheld them. I couldn't cancel the order if I wished. What would you think of a king who left his army in the lurch?"

"Nobody will ever accuse you of cowardice," Grim answered. "You're a proven brave man if ever there was one. The point is, do you want all your bravery and hard work for the Arab cause to go for nothing? Do you want the prospect of Arab independence to go up in smoke on a gas-swept battlefield?"

"It would break my heart," said Feisul, "although one heart hardly matters."

"It would break more hearts than yours," Grim retorted. "There are millions looking to you for leadership. Leave me out of it. Leave Lawrence out of it, and all the other non-Moslems who have done their bit for you. Leave most of these Syrians out of it; for they're simply politicians making use of you--a mess of breeds and creeds so mixed and corrupted that they don't know which end up they stand! If the Syrians had guts they'd have rallied so hard to you long ago that no outsider would have had a chance."

"What do you mean? What are you proposing?" Feisul asked quietly.

"Baghdad is your place, not Damascus!"

"But here I am in Damascus," Feisul retorted; and for the first time there was a note of impatience in his voice. "I came here at the request of the Allies, on the strength of their promises. I did not ask to be king. I would rather not be. Let any man be ruler whom the Arabs choose, and I will work for him loyally. But the Arabs chose me and the Allies consented. It was only after they had won their war with our help that the French began raising objections and, the British deserted me. It is too late to talk of Baghdad now."

"It isn't! It's too soon!" Grim answered, bringing down a clenched fist on his knee, and Feisul laughed in spite of himself.

"You talk like a prophet, Jimgrim, but let me tell you something. It is mainly a question of money after all. The British paid us a subsidy until they withdrew from Syria. They did their best for us even then, for they left behind guns, ammunition, wagons and supplies. When the French seized the ports they promised to continue the subsidy, because they are collecting the customs dues and we have no other revenue worth mentioning. But rather than send us money the French have told our people not to pay taxes; so our treasury is empty. Nevertheless, we contrived by one means and another. We arranged a bank credit, and ordered supplies from abroad. The supplies have reached Beirut, but the French have ordered the bank to cancel the credit, and until we pay for the supplies they are withheld."

"Any gas masks among the supplies you ordered?" Grim asked him; and Feisul nodded.

"That banker has played fast and loose with us until the last minute. Relying on our undertaking not to molest foreigners he has resided in Damascus, making promises one day and breaking them the next, keeping his funds in Beirut and his agency here, draining money out of the country all the while."

"Why didn't you arrest him?"

"We gave our word to the French that he should have complete protection and immunity. It seemed a good thing to us to have such an influential banker here; he has international connections. As recently as yesterday, twenty minutes before that ultimatum came, he was in this room assuring me that he would be able to solve the credit difficulty within a day or two."

"Would you like to send for him now?" suggested Grim.

"I doubt if he would come."

"Well, have him fetched!"

Feisul shook his head.

"If other people break their promises, that is no reason why we should break ours. If we can defeat the French and force them to make other terms, then we will expel him from Syria. I leave at midnight, Jimgrim."

"To defeat the French? You go to your Waterloo! You're in check with only one move possible, and I'm here to make you realize it. You're a man after my own heart, Feisul, but you and your Arabs are children at dealing with these foreign exploiters!

"They can beat you at every game but honesty. And listen: If you did defeat the French--if you drove them into the sea tomorrow, they'd get away with all the money in Beirut and you'd still be at the mercy of foreign capitalists! Instead of an independent Arab kingdom here you'd have a mixture of peoples and religions all plotting against one another and you, with capitulations and foreign consuls getting in the way, and bond-holding bankers sitting on top of it all like the Old Man of the Sea in the story of Sindbad the Sailor!

"Leave that to the French! Let them have all Syria to stew in! Go to England where your friends are. Let the politicians alone. Meet real folk and talk with them.

Tell them the truth; for they don't know it! Talk with the men and women who haven't got political jobs to lose--with the fellows who did the fighting--with the men and women who have votes. They'll believe you. They've given up believing politicians, and they're learning how to twist the politicians' tails. You'll find yourself in Baghdad within a year or two, with all Mesopotamia to make a garden of and none but Arabs to deal with. That's your field!"

Feisul smiled with the air of a man who recognizes but is unconvinced.

"There are always things that might have been," he answered. "As it is, I cannot desert the army."

"We'll save what we can of the army," Grim answered. "Your Syrians will save their own skins; it's only the Arabs we've got to look out for--a line of retreat for the Arab regiments, and another for you. It's not too late, and you know I'm right! Come on; let's get busy and do it!"

Feisul's smile was all affection and approval, but he shook his head.

"If what you say is true, I should only have the same problem in Mesopotamia--foreign financiers," he answered.

"That's exactly where you're wrong!" Grim retorted triumphantly.

He stood up, and pointed at Jeremy.

"Here's a man who owns a gold-mine. It lies between Mesopotamia and your father's kingdom of the Hedjaz, and its exact whereabouts is a secret. He's here tonight to make you a pres ent of the mine! And here's another man,"--he pointed at me--"a mining expert, who'll tell you what the thing's worth. It's yours, if you'll agree to abandon Syria and lay a course for Baghdad!"

## CHAPTER XIV

"You'll be a virgin Victim!"

Feisul was interested; he couldn't help being. And he was utterly convinced of Grim's sincerity. But he wasn't moved from his purpose, and not even Jeremy's account of the gold-mine, or my professional opinion of its value, had the least effect toward cancelling the plans he had in mind. He was deeply affected by the offer, but that was all.

"Good heavens, man!" Grim exploded suddenly. "Surely you won't throw the whole world into war again! You know what it will mean if the French kill or imprison you. There isn't a Moslem of all the millions in Asia who won't swear vengeance against the West--you know that! A direct descendant of Mohammed, and the first outstanding, conquering Moslem since Saladin--"

"The Allies should have thought of that before they broke promises," said Feisul.

"Never mind them. Damn them!" answered Grim. "It's up to you! The future of civilization is in your lap this minute! Can't you see that if you lose you'll be a martyr, and Islam will rise to avenge you?"

"Inshallah," said Feisul, nodding.

"But that if you let pride go by the board, and seem to run away, there'll be a breathing spell? Asia would wonder for a few months, and do nothing, until it began to dawn on them that you had acted wisely and had a better plan in view."

"I am not proud, except of my nation," Feisul answered. "I would not let pride interfere with policy. But it is too late to talk of this."

"Which is better?" Grin demanded. "A martyr, the very mention of whose name means war, or a living power for peace under a temporary cloud?"

"I am afraid I am a poor host.  Forgive me," Feisul answered.  "Dinner has been waiting all this while, and you have a lady with you.  This is disgraceful."

He rose and led the way into another room, closing the discussion.  We ate an ordinary meal in an ordinary dining room, Feisul presiding and talking trivialities with Mabel and Hadad.  There was an occasional boisterous interlude by Jeremy, but even he with his tales of unknown Arabia couldn't lift the load of depression.  Grim and I sat silent through the meal.  I experienced the sensation that you get when an expedition proves a failure and you've got to go home again with nothing done--all dreary emptiness;  but Grim was hatching something, as you could tell by the far-away expression and the glowering light in his eyes.  He looked about ready for murder.

Narayan Singh's face all through the meal was a picture--delight and pride at dining with a king, amazement at his karma that had brought a sepoy of the line to hear such confidences first hand, chagrin over Grim's apparent failure and desire to be inconspicuous controlled his expression in turn.  Once or twice he tried to make conversation with me, but I was in no mood for it, being a grouchy old bear on occasion without decent manners.

Feisul excused himself the minute the meal was over, saying he had a conference to attend, and we all went back into the sitting-room, where Grim took the chair he occupied before and marshalled us into a row on the seat in front of him.  He was back again in form--electric--and self-controlled.

"Have you folk got the hang of this?" he asked.  "Do you realize what it means if Feisul goes out and gets scuppered?"

We thought we did, even if we didn't.  I don't suppose anyone except the few who, like Grim, have made a life-study of the problem of Islam in all its bearings could quite have grasped it.  Mabel had a viewpoint that served Grim's purpose as well as any at the moment.

"That man's too good, and much too good-looking to be wasted!" she said emphatically.  "D'you suppose that if Colonel Lawrence were really here--"

"Half a minute," said Grim, "and I'll come to that.  How about you, Hadad?  How far would you go to save Feisul from this Waterloo?"

"I would go a long way," he answered cautiously.  "What do you intend?"

"To appear near the firing-line, for one thing, with somebody who looks like

Colonel Lawrence, and somebody else who looks enough like Feisul in one of Feisul's cars, and give the French a run for it in one direction while Feisul escapes in the other."

"Wallahi! But what if Feisul won't go?"

"He'll get helped! Did you ever hear what they did to Napoleon at Waterloo? Seized his bridle and galloped away with him."

"You mean I'm to act Lawrence again?" asked Mabel, looking deathly white. Grim nodded.

"Who's cast for Feisul?" Jeremy inquired.

"You are. You're the only trained stage-actor in the bunch. You're his height--not unlike his figure--"

"I resemble him as much as a kangaroo looks like an ostrich!" laughed Jeremy. "You're talking wild, Jim. What have you had to drink?"

"How about you, Ramsden? Will you see this through?"

Jeremy shook his head at me. I believe he thought for the moment that Grim had gone mad. He hadn't the experience of Grim that I had, and consequently not the same confidence in Grim's ability to dream, catch the essence of the dream, pin it down and make a fact of it.

"I'll go the limit," said I.

"Well, I'll be damned" laughed Jeremy. "All right; same here. I stake a gold-mine and Rammy raises me. Fetch your crown and sceptre and I'll play king to Jim's ace in a royal straight flush. Mabel's queen. Hadad's a knave. He looks it! Keep smiling, Hadad, old top, and I'll let you forgive me. Rammy's the ten-spot--tentative--tenacious--ten aces up his sleeve--and packs a ten-ton wallop when you get him going. What's Narayan Singh? The deuce?"

"The joker," answered Grim. "Are you in on this?"

"Sahib, there was no need to ask. What your honor finds good enough-- your honor's order--"

"Orders have nothing to do with it. We're not in British territory. This in unofficial. I've no right to give you orders," said Grim. "You're free to refuse. I'm likely to lose my job over this and so are you if you take part in it."

Narayan Singh grinned hugely.

"Hah! A sepoy's position is a smaller stake than a major's commission or a gold-mine, but I likewise have a life to lose, and I play too!"

Grim nodded curtly. It was no time for returning compliments.

"How about you, Mabel? We can manage this without you, and you've a husband to think of--"

"If he were here he'd hate it, but he'd give permission."

"All right. Now, Hadad. What about it?"

"Am I to obey you absolutely, not knowing what the--"

Grim interrupted him:

"The proposal's fair. Either you withdraw now and hold your tongue, or come in with us. If you're in I'll tell the details; if not, there's no need."

"Wallahi! What a sword-blade you are, Jimgrim! If I say 'yes,' I risk my future on your backgammon board; if I say 'no,' my life is worth a millieme, for you will tell that Sikh you call the 'joker' to attend to me!"

"Not so," Grim answered. "If you don't like the plan, I'll trust you to fall out and keep the secret."

"Oh, in that case," answered Hadad, hesitating. "Since you put it that way... well, it is lose all or perhaps win something--half-measures are no good--the alternative is ruin of the Arab cause--it is a forlorn hope--well, one throw of the dice, eh?--and all our fortunes on the table!--one little mistake and helas--finish! Never mind. Yes, I will play too. I will play this to the end with you."

"So we're all set," remarked Grim with a sigh of relief. Instantly he threw his shoulders back and began to set his pieces for the game. And you know, there's a world of difference between the captain of a side who doesn't worry until the game begins and Grim's sort, who do their worrying beforehand and then play, and make the whole side play for every ounce that's in them.

"Mabel, you're Lawrence. Keep silent, be shy, avoid encounters--act like a man who's not supposed to be here, but who came to help Feisul contrary to express commands laid on him by the Foreign Office. Get that? Lawrence is a shy man, anyway--hates publicity, rank, anything that calls attention to himself. The more shy you are, the easier you'll get away with it. Feisul must help pretend you're Lawrence. The presence of Lawrence would add to his prestige incalculably, and I think he'll see that, but if not, never mind, we'll manage. Any questions? Quick!"

You can't ask questions when you're given that sort of opportunity. The right ones don't occur to you and the others seem absurd. Grim knew that, of course, but when you're dealing with a woman there's just one chance in a hundred that she may think of something vital that hasn't occurred to anybody else. Most women aren't practical; but it's the impractical things that happen.

"Suppose we're captured by the French?" she suggested. "That's what's going to happen," he answered. "When they've got you, then you're Mrs. Mabel Ticknor, who never saw Lawrence and wouldn't recognize him if you did."

"They'll ask why I'm wearing man's clothes, and masquerading as an Arab."

"Well, you're a woman, aren't you? You answer with another question-- ask them just how safe a woman would be! They may claim that their Algerians are baby-lambs, but they can't blame you for not believing it! Anything else?"

She shook her head, and he turned on Hadad.

"Hadad, lose no opportunity of whispering that Lawrence is with Feisul. Add that Lawrence doesn't want his presence known. Hunt out two or three loyal Arabs on the staff and tell them the plan is to kidnap Feisul and carry him to safety across the border; but don't do it too soon; wait until the debacle begins, and then per-suade a few of them-- old Ali, for instance, and Osman--choose the old guard--you and they bolt with him to Haifa. The Syrians have been thoroughly undermined by propaganda; gas will do the rest, and as soon as the Arabs see the Syrians run they'll listen to reason. They know you, and know you're on the level. Do you un-derstand? Will you do that?"

"I will try. I see many a chance of spilling before this cup comes to the drink-ing, Jimgrim!"

"Then carry it carefully!" Grim answered. "Ramsden, take that car you came in. Find that banker. He's the boy who has bought Feisul's staff, or I'm much mis-taken. Bring him here." "Suppose he won't come?"

"Bring him. Take Jeremy with you. Try diplomacy first. Tell him that a plot to kidnap Feisul has been discovered at the last minute, but give him to understand that no suspicion rests on him. Get him, if you can, to send a message to the French General Staff, warning them to watch for Feisul and two civilians and Lawrence in an auto. After that bring him if you have to put him in a sack."

"What's his name, and where does he live?"

"Adolphe Rene. Everybody knows his house. Jeremy, look as unlike Feisul as you can until the time comes, but study the part and be ready to jump into his clothes. Narayan Singh, stay with me. You and I will do the dirty work. Get busy, Ramsden."

Circumstances work clock-fashion, wheel fitting into wheel, when those tides that Shakespeare spoke of are at flood. Disregarding all the theory and argument about human will as opposed to cosmic law I say this, without any care at all who contradicts me:

That whoever is near the hub of happenings is the agent of Universal Law, and can no more help himself than can the watch that tells the hour. The men who believe that they make history should really make a thoughtful fellow laugh. "The moving finger writes, and having writ moves on"; the old tentmaker Omar knew the truth of it. You could almost hear the balance-wheel of Progress click as the door opened before Grim had finished speaking, and a staff officer appeared to invite him to be present at Feisul's conference.

Grim asked at once for the auto for me (I couldn't have had it otherwise), and a moment later Jeremy and I were scooting into darkness through narrow streets and driving rain, with the hubs of the wheels awash in places and "shipping it green" over the floor when we dipped and pitched over a cross-street gutter. The Arab driver knew the way, from which I take it he had a compass in his head as well as a charm against accidents and a spirit of recklessness that put faith in worn-out springs. There wasn't room for more than one set of wheels at a time in most of the streets we tore through, but a camel tried to share one fairway with us and had the worst of it; he cannoned off into an alley 'hime end first, and we could hear him bellowing with rage a block away.

And our manner of stopping was like our progress, prompt. The brake-bands went on with a shriek and Jeremy and I pitched forward as the car brought up against the kerb in front of an enormous door, whose brass knocker shone like gold in the rays of our headlights. We told the Arab to wait for us and stepped knee-deep into a pool invisible, stumbled and nearly fell over a great stone set to bridge the flood between street and door, then proceeded to use the knocker importunately, thunderously, angrily, as men with wet feet and bruised toes likely will, whatever the custom of the country.

We went on knocking, taking turns, until the door opened at last and the banker's servant peered at us with a candle in his hand, demanding to know in the name of the thousand and one devils whom Solomon boiled in oil what impudent scavengers were making all that noise. But the banker himself was in the background, thinking perhaps that the French had come already, on the lookout over the servant's shoulder for a glimpse of a kepi. So we put our shoulders to the door, thrust by the servant, and walked in.

"Take care! I have a pistol in my hand!" said the banker's voice.

"Three shots for a shilling at me then!" retorted Jeremy.

"Who are you?"

"Tell that shivering fool to bring the candle, and you'll see!"

"Oh, you, is it! I told you to come in the morning. I can't see you now."

"Can't see me, eh? Come in here and peel your eyes, cocky! Sit down and look at us. There, take a pew. Wonder where I learned such good English? Well, I used to shine the toenails of the Prince o' Wales, and you have to pass a Civil Service examination before they give you that good job. I talk any language except French and Jewish, but this master of mine turns out to be a Jew who talks French, and not a prizefighter after all.

"What did I tell you this evening? Said he was a spy for the French, didn't I? I tell you, I'm a dependable man. What I say you can bet on till you've lost all your money. Here he is, spying to beat the promised-landers--just had tea with Feisul and learned all the inside facts--offered me a pound to come and find you, but I charged him two and got the money in advance.

"You ought to pay me a commission, too, and then I'll get married if there's an honest woman left in Damascus. If either of you want my advice, you won't believe a word the other says, but I expect you're both too wilful to be guided. Anyhow, you'll have to talk in front of me, because my master is afraid of being murdered; he isn't afraid of ghosts or bad smells, but the sight of a long knife turns his heart to water and sets him to praying so loud that you can't get a word in edgewise. Go on, both of you--yalla! Talk!"

Does it begin to be obvious why kings used to employ court jesters? The modern cabinets should have them--men like Jeremy (though they'd be hard to find) to break the crust of situations. Suspicion weakens in the presence of incongruity.

"This fellow seems less than half-witted," I said, "but he's shrewd, and I've found him useful. Unfortunately he has picked up a lot of information, so we'll have to keep an eye on him. My business is to communicate with the French General Staff and I'm told you know how to manage it."

"Huh-huh? Who told you that?"

"Those who gave me my instructions. If you don't know who they are without my telling you, you're the wrong man and I'll not waste time with you."

"Let us suppose that I know then. Proceed."

"Your name was given to me as that of a man who can be trusted to take necessary action in the interests of ... er ... you understand?"

"Uh-huh!"

"The plot for Feisul to be kidnapped by some Syrian members of his staff has been discovered at the last minute," I said, looking hard at him; and he winced palpably.

"Mon Dieu! You mean--"

"That it is not too late to save the situation. You have not been accused of connection with it. I came here in pursuance of a different plan to kidnap him--a sort of reserve plan, to be employed in case other means should fail. All arrangements are in working order except the one item of communicating with the French General Staff. I require you to accompany me for that purpose, and to send off to them immediately a message at my dictation."

"Tschaa! Suppose you show me your authority?"

"Certainly!" I answered.

Realizing that he wasn't in immediate danger of life he had returned his own pistol to his pocket. So I showed him the muzzle of mine, and he divined without a sermon on the subject that it would go off and shoot accurately unless he showed discretion. He didn't offer to move when Jeremy's agile fingers found his pocket and flicked out the mother-of- pearl-handled, rim-fire thing with which he had previously kept his courage warm.

"I was told not to trust you too far," I explained. "I was warned in advance that you might question my credentials. You are said to be jealous of interference. As a precaution against miscarriage of this plan through jealousy on your part, I was ordered to oblige you to obey me."

"And if I refuse?"

"Your widow will then be the individual most concerned. Be good enough to take pen and paper, and write a letter to my dictation."

Jeremy went to the door, which was partly open, made sure that the servant was out of earshot, and slammed it tight. Rene the banker went to his escritoire, took paper, and shook his fountain pen.

"How shall I commence the letter?" he asked me with a dry, sly smile.

He thought he had me there. There are doubtless proper forms of address that serve to establish the genuineness of letters written by a spy.

"Commence half-way down the page," I answered. "We'll insert the address afterwards. Write in French:"

"I shall accompany the Emir Feisul and Colonel Lawrence to the front tonight, former plan having miscarried. When Syrian retreat begins look out for automobile containing Feisul and Lawrence, which may be recognized easily as it will also contain myself and another civilian in plain clothes. At the psychological moment a white flag will be shown from it, waved perhaps surreptitiously by one of the civilians. In the event of breakdown of the automobile a horsed vehicle will be used and the same signal will apply. For the sake of myself and the other civilian, please instruct all officers to keep a sharp lookout and protect the party from being fired on."

"There," I said, "sign that and address it."

He hesitated. He couldn't doubt that his own arrangements with traitors on the staff to kidnap Feisul had gone amiss, else how should I be aware of them at all--I, who had only arrived that evening in Damascus? But it puzzled him to know why I should make him write the letter, or, since his plan must have failed, why I should let him share in the kidnapping. He smelt the obvious rat. Why didn't I sign the letter myself, and get all the credit afterward, as any other spy would do?

"You sign it," he said, pushing the letter toward me; and I got one of those sudden inspirations that there is no explaining--the right idea for handling fox Rene the banker.

"So you're afraid to sign that, are you? All right; give it here, I'll sign it; pass me your pen. But you'll come along with me tonight, my lad, and make your explanations to the French in the morning!"

Looking back, I can see how the accusation worked, although it was an arrow shot at a venture. His greasy, sly, fox face with its touch of bold impudence betrayed him for a man who would habitually hedge his bets. Feisul's safe-conduct had protected him from official interference, but it had needed more than that to preserve him from unofficial murder, and beyond a doubt he had betrayed the French in minor ways whenever that course looked profitable. Now in a crisis he had small choice but to establish himself as loyal to the stronger side. He hurriedly wrote a number at the bottom of the letter, and another followed by three capitals and three more figures at the top.

"Seal it up and send it--quick!" I ordered him.

He obeyed and Jeremy called the servant.

"Summon Francois," said the banker, and the servant disappeared again.

Francois must remain a mystery. He was insoluble. Dressed in a pair of baggy Turkish pants, with a red sash round his middle, knotted loosely over a woollen jersey that had wide horizontal black and yellow strips, with a grey woollen shawl over the lot, and a new tarboosh a size or two too small for him perched at an angle on his head, he stood shifting from one bare foot to the other and moved a toothless gap in his lower face in what was presumably a smile.

He had no nose that you could recognize, although there were two blow- holes in place of nostrils with a hideous long scar above them. One ear was missing. He had no eyebrows. But the remaining ear was pointed at the top like a satyr's, and his little beady eyes were as black as a bird's and inhumanly bright.

The banker spoke to him in the voice you would use to a rather spoilt child when obedience was all-important, using Arabic with a few French words thrown in.

"Ah, here is Francois. Good Francois! Francois, mon brave, here is a letter, eh? You know where to take it--eh? Ha-ha! Francois knows, doesn't he! Francois doesn't talk; he tells nobody; he's wise, is Francois! He runs, eh? He runs through the rain and the night; and he hides so that nobody can see him; and he delivers the letter; and somebody gives Francois money and tobacco and a little rum; and Francois comes running back to the nice little, dark little hole where he sleeps. Plenty to eat, eh, Francois? Nice soft food that needs no chewing! Nothing to do but run with a letter now and then, eh? A brave fellow is Francois--a clever fellow--a trustworthy fellow--a dependable, willing fellow, always ready to please! Ready to go?

"Well, there's the letter; be careful with it, and run-run-run like a good boy! A whole bottle of rum when you come back--think of it! A whole bottle of nice brown rum to yourself in that nice little room where your bed is! There, goodbye!"

The creature addressed as Francois vanished, with a snort and a sort of squeal that may have been meant for speech. "That is the best messenger in Syria," said Rene. "He is priceless--incorruptible, silent, and as sure as Destiny! The French General Staff will have that letter before dawn. Now--what next?"

"You come with me," I answered.

He felt better now that the message was on its way; second thought convinced him of my connection with the French. There is no more profitless delusion than to suppose that a country's secret agents are always its own nationals. They are almost always not.

If the French used only Frenchmen, Germany used none but Germans, Great Britain only Englishmen, and so on, it might be prettier and easier for the police, but intelligence departments would starve. So there was nothing about an obvious American doing spy-work for the French that should stick in his craw; and that being so, the more cheerfully he aided me the better it would likely be for him.

So he called for the servant again, and proved himself a good campaigner by superintending the packing of a big basket with provisions--bread and butter, cold chicken, wine, olives, and hot coffee in a thermos bottle.

"The French will be in Damascus by noon tomorrow," he said. "Ha-ha! Those French and their hungry Algerians! We do well to take a good provision with us-- enough for two days at least. We shall enter with them, I suppose, or at least behind them, and of course my house here will receive consideration; but--ha-ha!--how many chickens do you believe will be purchasable in Damascus one hour after the first Algerians get here? Eh? Put in another chicken, Hassan, mon brave. Eh bien, oui--pack the basket full; put in more of everything!"

At last he got into an overcoat lined with fox-pelt, for the night air was chilly and an overcoat is less trouble than blankets if you expect to spend a night on the move. We hove the huge basket into the waiting auto, slammed the front door of the house behind us, piled into the back seat and were off.

"I shall be glad when this business is over," said Rene, with a sigh of satisfaction. "I am a banker by profession. For me the ebb and flow of trade, with its certainties and its discretions. But what would you? Trade must be prepared for; doors that will not open must be forced; those who stand in the way must be thrust aside. This Feisul is an impossible fellow. He is a hypocrite, I tell you--one of those praters about righteousness who won't understand that the church and the mosque are the places for that sort of thing. Eh? You follow me? But tell me, what has been done to Daulch, Hattin and Aubek? Were they backed against a wall and shot? Who betrayed them? Too bad that such a plan should fail, for it was perfect."

"Far from perfect," I answered; for that one piece of strategy I have by heart--the way to make a man tell all he knows is to pretend to superior knowledge.

"Heh? How could you improve on it? Three members of the staff to order sauve-qui-peut unexpectedly, seize Feisul, and deliver him dead or alive? What is better than that? But what has been done to the three?"

"Nothing," I answered.

"Just like him! just like him! I tell you, that man Feisul would rather be a martyr than succeed at his proper business." We reached the palace just as Feisul was leaving it. Several members of his staff were hard on his heels in the porch and our party was behind them again, with Mabel last of all. There was a line of waiting autos nearly long enough to fill the drive, but an utter absence of military fuss, and no shouting or hurry. It looked in the dark more like a funeral than the departure of a king to join his army at the front.

I remained in the car with the banker and sent Jeremy to report our doings to Grim. Presently I could see him standing under the porch lamp with a hand on Grim's shoulder, and I leaned out over the auto door to watch; but Rene the banker leaned back, snuggled up in his overcoat, liking neither to be seen nor to get his skin wet. I expected to see the three staff officers Daulch, Hattin and Aubek arrested there and then; but nothing happened, except that Feisul suddenly drove away with Mabel and Grim in the same car with him.

There followed a rush for the other cars, and the whole line started forward, Jeremy jumping in as our car passed the porch. "Daulch, Hattin and Aubek are at the front," he said, and began humming to himself.

"At the front?" demanded Rene, sitting upright suddenly. "At the front, you say? When did they leave for the front?"

"This evening," answered Jeremy.

You couldn't see his face in the dark, but I think he was chuckling.

"Strange!" said the banker. "Yet you say they have been betrayed--their plan is known--yet they left for the front this evening?"

It was pitch-dark inside the car, for the rain swished down in torrents and Jeremy fastened the flaps after he got in. Rene's change of expression was a thing that you could feel, not see. He kept perfect silence for about two minutes, while the car skidded and bumped at the rear of the procession. Then:

"You tell me that Feisul knows, and yet..."

"Oh, I didn't tell you that," laughed Jeremy. "It was this other man who said so. I never deceived anyone; I'm an honest fellow, I am. Remember, I warned you against him when we talked in the hotel; you can't blame me. I told you he was up to mischief. I advised you to keep a careful eye on him and to look twice at his paper! Wallah! You must be a lamb in foxskin. My master is a wolf in a woolly overcoat! Wait till you've seen him eat that chicken that you brought, and then you'll know what kind of a man he is!

"You see, you should have given me money when I asked you for it. I'm a fellow with a price, I am. Whoever pays my price gets his money's worth. If you'd had the sense to pay me more than this man does, I'd have helped you trick him instead of helping him trick you; but he gave me my wages before dinner and you gave me nothing, so here you are, and I wouldn't like to be keeping your pair of trousers warm! I tell you, this Ramsden effendi is an awful fellow, who will stick at nothing, and I'm worse because I'm honest and do what I'm paid to do!"

I took the precaution of putting my arm around Rene, for it was likely that he had another weapon hidden somewhere, and the obvious thing for him to do was to shoot the two of us and make a bolt for it. For a second I thought I felt his hand moving; but it was Jeremy's, searching all his pockets and feeling for hidden steel. So I pulled out a cigar and lit a match.

Of course, anyone's face looks ghastly by that sort of sudden light; but Rene's was a picture of hate, rage, baffled cunning and fear, such as I had never seen; his eyes looked like an animal's at bay, and the way his lips parted from his teeth conveyed the impression that he was searching his mind wildly for a desperate remedy that would ruin all concerned except himself.

But it was only a stale old recourse that he had. In a man's extremity he turns by instinct to his own tin gods for help, and you may read his whole heart and religion then.

"Very well; very well," he said, as if he were on the rack, speaking hurriedly to get it over with. "I make the sacrifice. You will find my money in an inner vest pocket underneath my vest. It is a life's savings. Take it, and let me go. It is not much--only a little--I am not a rich man--I had hoped to be, but it would mean a fortune to you no doubt. Take it and be merciful; give me back the smaller packet of the two, keep the larger, and let me go."

Out of curiosity I reached inside his vest and pulled out both packets. Jeremy struck a match. The smaller packet contained a draft on Paris for a quarter of a million francs. The larger held nothing but correspondence. I returned them to him.

"Listen!" I said. "I've never yet murdered a man, so if you provide me with another excuse for murdering you, you'll be a virgin victim. Keep that in mind!"

---

# CHAPTER XV

"Catch the Alfies napping and kick hell out of 'em!"

You're no doubt familiar with the fact that the accounts given by two men who have witnessed a battle from the same angle will differ widely, not only in minor detail but in fundamentals; so you won't look to me for confirmation of any one of the countless stories that have seen the light of print, pretending to explain how the French won Damascus so easily and unexpectedly. I was only on the inside, looking outward as it were; the fellows on the outside, looking in, would naturally give a different explanation.

Then you must bear in mind that this is a day of "official" accounts that would make a limping dog of Ananias. When the General Staff of an invading army controls all the wires and all lines of communication you may believe what they choose to tell you, if you wish. But you don't have to, as they say in Maine. And I admit that all I saw was from a curtained auto as we swayed and bumped over broken roads, with an occasional interlude when Jeremy and I got out to lend our shoulders and help the Arab driver heave the car out of a slough.

My clearest memory is of that Arab--silent, stolid, staring like an owl straight forward most of the time--but a perfect marvel in emergencies, when he would suddenly spring to life, swear a living streak of brimstone blasphemy in high falsetto, and perform a driver's miracle.

By two flours after midnight we were running on four flat tires; and I've got the name of the maker of those wheels for future reference and use. One spring broke, but we went forward sailor-fashion, with a jury- rig of chain and rope, after getting more gas from some Christian monks, who swore they hadn't any and wept when one of Feisul's officers demonstrated that they lead. You couldn't see any monastery; I don't even know that there was one--nothing but lean faces with tonsured tops that nodded in unison and lied fearfully.

The gunfire began to be heavy about that time, although nothing like the thousand-throated bedlam of Flanders. As neither side could see the other and neither had any ranges marked, my guess is that the French were advertising their advance--doing a little propaganda that was cheap for all concerned except the tax-payers. And the Syrian army was shooting back crazily, sending over long shots on the off chance, more to encourage themselves than for any other reason.

The sensation was rather like riding in an ambulance away from the battle instead of toward it, for you couldn't see anything and you had a sense of helpless detachment from it all, as if a power you couldn't control were carrying you away from a familiar destiny to one that you couldn't imagine. It wasn't so much like a dream as like a different, real existence that you couldn't understand because it bore no kind of relation to anything in the past.

Anyhow, we bumped and blundered on until dawn came, streaked with wonderful rolling mist, and gave a glimpse at intervals of a wide plain sloping toward the west, with long lines of infantry and here and there guns extended across it in parallels drawn north and south.

The rifle firing started ten minutes after dawn, and it was all over in less than half an hour; but I can't describe exactly how the finish came, because the wind was toward us and the morning mist blew along in blanketing white masses that only allowed you a momentary glimpse and then shut off the view.

We were about a mile behind the firing-line and I couldn't see Feisul's car or any of the others. For the moment there was just one clear line of vision, straight from where I sat to the nearest infantry. I could see about fifty yards of the line and perhaps that many men; and they were blazing away furiously over a low earthwork, although I couldn't see a sign of the French. There was hardly any artillery firing at that time.

Suddenly without any obvious reason the men whose backs I was watching broke and ran. The mist obscured them instantly and the line of vision shifted, so that bit by bit I saw I dare say a mile of the firing line. The whole lot were running for their lives and, look where I would, there wasn't a sign of a Frenchman anywhere.

I should say it took about ten minutes for the first of them to reach the dirt road, where our autos stood hub-deep in mud, and by that time we had shoved and pulley-hauled them into movement, our engines making as much row as a nest of machine-guns as they struggled against the strain. We didn't want to be swamped under that tide of fugitives.

But they took no notice of us. They had thrown away their weapons and were running for home with eyes distended and nothing in mind but to put distance between there and the enemy. I jumped out of the car and seized one man.

"What are you running from? What has happened?" I demanded, holding him harder the more he struggled.

"Poison gas!" he gasped, and I let him go.

I thought I caught a whiff of the darned stuff then, but that may have been imagination.

"Poison gas!" I said, returning to the car, and Rene made a fine exhibition of himself, smothering his head under the foxlined overcoat and screaming.

He got right down on the floor of the car and lay there huddled and gasping-- which may have been a sensible precaution; I don't know. There was no time just then to bother with him.

The flukey morning breeze shifted several points. The mist curled suddenly and began to flow diagonally across our line of cars instead of toward us, and from one moment to the next you could see straight along the road for maybe a mile or more. There was a sight worth seeing-- Feisul's cavalry in full rout--running away from ghosts by the look of it--their formation hardly yet broken, horse and man racing with the wind and a scattering of unhorsed fugitives streaming behind like a comet's tail.

According to Grim, who should know, that cavalry division was the kingpin of Feisul's plan. He had intended to lead a raid in person, swooping down the French flank to their rear; but the three staff traitors, Daulch, Hattin and Aubck, sent forward the previous evening to place the division and hold it ready, had simply tipped the French off to the whole plan and at the critical moment of Feisul's arrival on the scene had ordered the sauve-qui-peut. I don't believe the French used more than a can or two of gas. I don't believe they had more than a few cans of it so far advanced.

But the sauve-qui-peut might have been useless without Feisul's capture, for he was just the man to rally a routed army and snatch victory out of a defeat. Nobody knew better than Feisul the weakness of the French communications, and the work of those three traitors was only half done when the cavalry took to its heels. The one man who could possibly save the day had to be bagged and handed over.

I didn't realize all that, of course, in the twinkling of an eye, as they say you do in a climax. Maybe I've never faced a climax. I'm no psychologist and not at all given to review of sudden situations in the abstract.

There was a fight, or a riot, or something like it going on near the head of our line of autos. The first two or three had come to a standstill; several in the middle of the line were trying to wheel outward and bolt for it behind the fleeing cavalry, and those at the tail end were blocked by one that had broken down. Of course everybody was yelling at the top of his lungs and the hurrying shreds of blown mist further confounded the confusion.

So Jeremy and I ran forward, plunging through the mud and knocking over whoever blocked our way. It was rather fun--like the football field at school. But one man--a Syrian officer--stood near the last of the forward cars with the evident purpose of standing off interference. He took careful aim at me with a revolver, fired point-blank, and missed.

I forgot all about my own pistol and went for him with a laugh and a yell of sheer exhilaration. There's an eighth of a ton of me, mostly bone and muscle, so it isn't a sinecure to have to stop my fist when the rest of the bulk is under way behind it. I landed so hard on his nose, and with such tremendous impetus, that he hadn't enough initial stability to take the impact and bring me up on my feet. He went down like a ninepin, I on top of him, laughing with mud in my teeth, and Jeremy landed on top of the two of us, holding the skirts of his cloak in both hands as he jumped.

Jeremy picked up the fellow's revolver and threw it out of sight, and the two of us ran on again--too late by now to help in the emergency, but in time for the next event.

Grim had managed everything, although he was bleeding, and smiling serenely through the blood. Hadad was there, not smiling at all, but bleached white with excitement; he had brought a number of Arab officers with him, six or seven of whom were standing on the running- board of the front car and all arguing with Feisul, who sat back with his feet and hands tied, guarded by Narayan Singh.

At Grim's feet--dead, with bullets through their heads--were three Syrian staff officers. They were the traitors Daulch, Hattin and Aubek. Grim's pistol was in his right hand and had been used.

There had been a first-class fight, all over in two minutes; for the traitors hadn't arrived on the scene without assistants. Unfortunately for them, Hadad had turned up at the same moment with his loyalists. Narayan Singh had jumped from the car behind and seized Feisul, thrown him to the floor out of the path of bullets, and tied his arms. It was actually Mabel, hardly realizing what she was doing but obeying the Sikh's orders yelled in her ear as he struggled to keep his wiry prisoner down, who tied the king's feet, using her Arab girdle.

Feisul, of course, was all for dying at the head of a remnant of his men. That would be the first impulse of any decent leader in like circumstance. But his loyal friends, eager to die with him if they must, but unwilling to die at all if there were an alternative, were overwhelming him with streams of words and promises. Suddenly two of them jumped into the car and began to untie his arms and feet. Grim, looking swiftly to right and left, saw Jeremy and pounced on him so fiercely that an onlooker might have guessed another fight to the death was under way. Too excited to say what he had in mind, he tugged at Jeremy's clothes.

"I get you, Jim--I get you!" Jeremy laughed gaily, and in ten seconds had stripped himself down to his underwear.

Hadad must have been discussing details of the plan with Grim along the road; for he got busy at the same time, persuading Feisul to part with his garments--not that his consent really mattered at the moment; they were pulled off him by half a dozen hands at once, and Jeremy had the best of that bargain all right, for in addition to silk headdress and a fine black Arab full-dress coat, there was linen of a sort you can't buy--better stuff than bishops wear and clean, which Jeremy's own wasn't.

The time it takes to read this gives a totally false impression of the speed. The whole thing took place, I should say, within two minutes from the time when I punched that Syrian's nose until Mabel and Narayan Singh stood beside me watching Hadad, two more Arabs and Feisul drive away, with a second car crowded full of loyalists in close attendance.

By that time Jeremy was dressed in Feisul's clothes; and though he didn't look a bit like Feisul from a yard away, in the mist at ten yards, provided you were looking for Feisul, you'd have taken your Bible oath he was the man; for he had the gesture and mannerism copied to perfection.

However, standing there wasn't going to increase the real Feisul's chance of escaping. The sooner we got caught, the quicker the French would discover that our man had given them the slip. Our business was to give the French a long chase in the wrong direction, and those bogged autos weren't ideal for the purpose.

But they were the only means in sight just then, and we had to bear in mind that message I had made Rene send, warning the French to look out for an auto with a white flag and two civilians together with Feisul and Lawrence. So we picked out the two best that remained, pitched Rene and his basket of provisions into the front one with Mabel and Jeremy, piled Narayan Singh in after them to take my place as the second civilian, and started them off straight forward, Grim and I following in a second car after I had paid our former Arab driver handsomely and sent him off grinning to give a lift to as many runaways as the car would hold.

We learned afterward that the rascal made a fortune, charging as much as fifty pounds sterling for the trip halfway back to Damascus, at which point the car collapsed. They say he carried eleven officers that far, bought two wives with the proceeds and escaped all the way to a village near Mecca, where his home was.

You know how bewildering and tricky those early mists are when they start to roll up before the wind. We had hardly got going when the whole mass seemed to shift in one great cloud, covering the fleeing troops and incidentally Feisul, but leaving us in our two autos high and dry, as it were, in full view of the French. And they were advancing by that time.

I couldn't see more than a division of them that we would have to reckon with--nearly all Algerians--and they looked dead-weary. I guess they had forced the pace in advance of the main body in order to take advantage of the treason of Feisul's officers. They came slouching forward with their rifles at the trail and a screen of skirmishers thrown out a quarter of a mile or so ahead.

There were cavalry and guns far off on their right, evidently trying to work around to the flank of the fleeing array, but those were much too far away to trouble us and were going in the wrong direction. Rolling banks of mist shut off the farther view to westward and there was no guessing where the main French force might be, and for all I know it hadn't started from the coast yet.

Fortune came to our rescue with one riderless horse, a splendid Arab gelding tied by the bridle to the wheel of a water-cart and left behind in the stampede. Jeremy appropriated it, riding Arab fashion with short stirrups, and I wouldn't have blamed Feisul's own brother for falsely identifying him at ten yards. He was born mischievous and he caricatured Feisul on horseback as if he were acting for the movies.

I guess the French officers had good glasses with them, for Jeremy had hardly mounted when the advancing Algerians opened a hot fire on us. The whole division surely wouldn't have blazed away, with machine-guns and all, at two cars and a man on horseback unless someone had passed the word along that Feisul was in full view.

So Grim and I abandoned our car, driver and all, and jumped into Jeremy's place. It wasn't more than two hundred yards to the top of a gentle rise, over which we disappeared from view; and just as we bumped over it I wrenched out the white tablecloth in which Rene's chicken and stuff was wrapped and waved it violently.

Then, Lord, what a sight! Below us, sheltered between two flanking hillocks, was about a division of Feisul's Arab infantry, packing up sulkily, preparing to follow the retreat. It was a safe bet the French didn't know they were there, and I dare say the same thought occurred to every one of us the same instant. Mabel thought of it. I know I did. But Jeremy voiced it first, heeling his horse up beside us.

"What do you say, Jim? I bet you I can rally that gang. Shall I lead 'em and lick hell out of the Algies?"

But Grim shook his head.

"You might, but the game is to pull the plug properly. Get this lot on the run. The less fighting, the less risk of drasticism when the French get to Damascus. Chase 'em off home!"

So Jeremy did it; and that, I believe, accounts for a story that got in the newspapers about Feisul trying to spring a surprise on the French at the last minute. Some French officers in armored cars came over the brow of the hill in pursuit of us--three cars, three officers, three machine-guns, and about a dozen men. One car quit on the hill-top, so I suppose it broke down, but its occupants must have seen Jeremy careering up and down the line encouraging those sulky Arabs to get a move on, and I suppose they told tales afterwards to a newspaper correspondent at the base.

Anyhow, the two pursuing armored cars didn't dare come near enough to be dangerous until we had followed the retreating Arab regiments for about a mile, and the Algerians appeared over the hill-top, coming very slowly. A long-range rifle-fire commenced, the Arabs returning it scrappily as they retreated; and we made believe there were other regiments to be shepherded, steering a northward course downhill toward broken ground that couldn't have suited our purpose better. By the way those armored cars came after us, keeping their distance, it was clear enough that they suspected an ambush.

So we had a clear start and led them a dance in and out among boulders and the branches of a watercourse, Jeremy galloping ahead to spy a course out. Whenever they came in view we acted a little piece for them, making Rene wave the white cloth while I protected him and held off Mabel and Grim, who went through the motions of trying to brain me with pistol butts.

Two or three times they opened fire, more by way of forcing a surrender, I think, than with any intention of hitting us; they wanted to take Feisul alive. It was like a game of fox and geese, and with Jeremy scouting ahead we could have kept them dodging us for hours if we hadn't run out of gas.

Then we abandoned the car and took refuge in a cave that stank as if it had been a tomb for generations. The French drew up their cars fifty yards away with machine-guns covering the cave mouth; and after we were sure they weren't going to squirt a stream of lead at us, I went out with the tablecloth to negotiate terms.

I didn't want to go, but Grim seemed to think they'd understand my French.

Of course, there wasn't anything really to argue about, but I played for time, because every minute was of value to the real Feisul, speeding on his way to British territory. The French officer who did the talking for his side--a little squat, pale, pug-faced fellow, who gave the impression of having risen from the ranks without learning polite manners on the way, agreed to accept our surrender and spare our lives for the time being; and by that time the smell in the cave had nearly overcome our party, so they all marched out.

And Lord! The French captain was spiteful when he discovered that Jeremy wasn't Feisul after all. He swore like a wet cat, accused Mabel of being a spy, took away our basket of provisions, and I think would have shot Jeremy out of hand if Jeremy hadn't started clowning and made the other Frenchmen laugh.

Laughter and murder no more mix than oil and water. He did what he called a harem dance for them, misusing his stomach outrageously, and the incongruity of that by a descendant of the Prophet took all the sting out of the situation. But they burned our abandoned car in sheer ill temper before crowding us into their own. And they shot the good horse.

The joy-ride that followed was rather like the kind they give pigs on the way to the sausage shop--hurried and not intended to be mirthful.

"What's the use of losing tempers?" I asked Captain Jacques Daudet, who had captured us.

He sat on my knees, with his pistol pressed against my chest. "Why not regard the whole thing as a joke? You've done your best and nobody can blame you. Besides, what can possibly happen? What do you suppose they'll do to us?"

He shrugged his shoulders and his little cold blue eyes met mine.

"You will all be shot, of course," he answered. "After that..."

He shrugged his shoulders again. But he cast no gloom; for Jeremy kept the lot of us, French too, excepting Daudet, in roars of laughter for ten miles until we reached temporary headquarters, where a born gentleman in a peaked red cap with gold on it sat on a camp-stool directing things.

He recognized Grim at the first glance and knew him for an American in British service. He looked Grim in the eye and smiled. We told our story in turns, interrupting one another and being interrupted by Rene. The officer turned on the banker savagely, ordered him sent to the rear, and smiled at Grim again.

Then he picked up the banker's belongings, including the two packages, and tossed them after him with an air of utter contempt.

Whereat he smiled at all of us.

"And you are quite sure that the Emir Feisul has escaped?" he asked.

"Well, there are those whom the news will annoy, which is too bad, but can't be helped. For myself, I cannot say that I shall shed tears. Madame..." He looked straight at Mabel. "Major..." He met Grim's eyes and smiled. "Messieurs ..." It was my turn, and Narayan Singh's; his steady stare was good and made you feel like shaking hands with him. "Monsieur Scapin (Clown)..." That was meant for Jeremy, and they both laughed. "You have been adroit, but do you think I could depend on your discretion?"

We did our best to look discreet.

"You see, Madame et Messieurs, this is not warfare. We desire to accomplish a definite object with as little unpleasantness as possible. I shall regret the necessity of sending you to Beirut, but that is for your safety. An additional and very sound precaution which you yourselves might take would be to preserve complete silence regarding the events of the last two days. Subject to that condition, you will be given facilities for leaving Beirut by sea in any direction you may wish. Do we understand one another? Good! Now, let me see whether I have your names correctly."

He carefully wrote them down all wrong, described us as noncombatants, who should be allowed to leave the country, warned Jeremy that in a king's clothes he looked too "intriguing," provided plain clothes for him, returned our belongings (except the basket of provisions, which he kept) and sent us off in an ambulance on the first leg of the journey to Beirut, whence we got away in a coastwise steamer within the week. "Not all the French are swabs!" said Jeremy grievously as we took our leave of him.

Grim agreed.

"Not all of 'em. Let's see--there was the Marne, the Aisne, the Somme, Verdun..."

### The Codes Of Hammurabi And Moses
### W. W. Davies

QTY

The discovery of the Hammurabi Code is one of the greatest achievements of archaeology, and is of paramount interest, not only to the student of the Bible, but also to all those interested in ancient history...

**Religion**     **ISBN: *1-59462-338-4***     **Pages:132**
*MSRP $12.95*

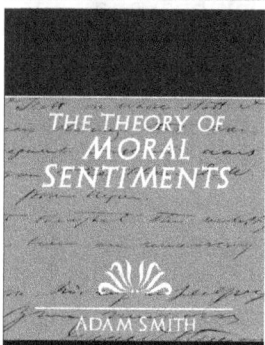

### The Theory of Moral Sentiments
### Adam Smith

QTY

This work from 1749. contains original theories of conscience amd moral judgment and it is the foundation for systemof morals.

**Philosophy  ISBN: *1-59462-777-0***     **Pages:536**
*MSRP $19.95*

### Jessica's First Prayer
### Hesba Stretton

QTY

In a screened and secluded corner of one of the many railway-bridges which span the streets of London there could be seen a few years ago, from five o'clock every morning until half past eight, a tidily set-out coffee-stall, consisting of a trestle and board, upon which stood two large tin cans, with a small fire of charcoal burning under each so as to keep the coffee boiling during the early hours of the morning when the work-people were thronging into the city on their way to their daily toil...

**Pages:84**
**Childrens    ISBN: *1-59462-373-2***     *MSRP $9.95*

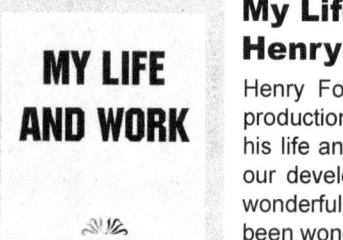

### My Life and Work
### Henry Ford

QTY

Henry Ford revolutionized the world with his implementation of mass production for the Model T automobile. Gain valuable business insight into his life and work with his own auto-biography... "We have only started on our development of our country we have not as yet, with all our talk of wonderful progress, done more than scratch the surface. The progress has been wonderful enough but..."

**Pages:300**
**Biographies/    ISBN: *1-59462-198-5***     *MSRP $21.95*

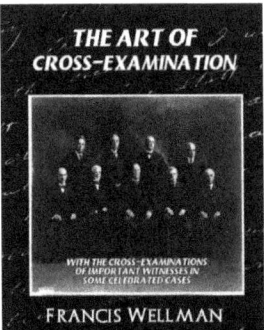

## The Art of Cross-Examination
## Francis Wellman

QTY

I presume it is the experience of every author, after his first book is published upon an important subject, to be almost overwhelmed with a wealth of ideas and illustrations which could readily have been included in his book, and which to his own mind, at least, seem to make a second edition inevitable. Such certainly was the case with me; and when the first edition had reached its sixth impression in five months, I rejoiced to learn that it seemed to my publishers that the book had met with a sufficiently favorable reception to justify a second and considerably enlarged edition. ..

**Pages:412**

Reference     ISBN: *1-59462-647-2*          *MSRP $19.95*

## On the Duty of Civil Disobedience
## Henry David Thoreau

QTY

Thoreau wrote his famous essay, On the Duty of Civil Disobedience, as a protest against an unjust but popular war and the immoral but popular institution of slave-owning. He did more than write—he declined to pay his taxes, and was hauled off to gaol in consequence. Who can say how much this refusal of his hastened the end of the war and of slavery ?

**Pages:48**

Law          ISBN: *1-59462-747-9*          *MSRP $7.45*

## Dream Psychology Psychoanalysis for Beginners
## Sigmund Freud

QTY

Sigmund Freud, born Sigismund Schlomo Freud (May 6, 1856 - September 23, 1939), was a Jewish-Austrian neurologist and psychiatrist who co-founded the psychoanalytic school of psychology. Freud is best known for his theories of the unconscious mind, especially involving the mechanism of repression; his redefinition of sexual desire as mobile and directed towards a wide variety of objects; and his therapeutic techniques, especially his understanding of transference in the therapeutic relationship and the presumed value of dreams as sources of insight into unconscious desires.

**Pages:196**

Psychology     ISBN: *1-59462-905-6*          *MSRP $15.45*

## The Miracle of Right Thought
## Orison Swett Marden

QTY

Believe with all of your heart that you will do what you were made to do. When the mind has once formed the habit of holding cheerful, happy, prosperous pictures, it will not be easy to form the opposite habit. It does not matter how improbable or how far away this realization may see, or how dark the prospects may be, if we visualize them as best we can, as vividly as possible, hold tenaciously to them and vigorously struggle to attain them, they will gradually become actualized, realized in the life. But a desire, a longing without endeavor, a yearning abandoned or held indifferently will vanish without realization.

**Pages:360**

Self Help          ISBN: *1-59462-644-8*          *MSRP $25.45*

**The Rosicrucian Cosmo-Conception Mystic Christianity** by *Max Heindel*     ISBN: *1-59462-188-8*   **$38.95**
*The Rosicrucian Cosmo-conception is not dogmatic, neither does it appeal to any other authority than the reason of the student. It is: not controversial, but is: sent forth in the, hope that it may help to clear...*                    New Age/Religion Pages 646

**Abandonment To Divine Providence** by *Jean-Pierre de Caussade*     ISBN: *1-59462-228-0*   **$25.95**
*"The Rev. Jean Pierre de Caussade was one of the most remarkable spiritual writers of the Society of Jesus in France in the 18th Century. His death took place at Toulouse in 1751. His works have gone through many editions and have been republished...*          Inspirational/Religion Pages 400

**Mental Chemistry** by *Charles Haanel*     ISBN: *1-59462-192-6*   **$23.95**
*Mental Chemistry allows the change of material conditions by combining and appropriately utilizing the power of the mind. Much like applied chemistry creates something new and unique out of careful combinations of chemicals the mastery of mental chemistry...*          New Age Pages 354

**The Letters of Robert Browning and Elizabeth Barret Barrett 1845-1846 vol II**     ISBN: *1-59462-193-4*   **$35.95**
by *Robert Browning* and *Elizabeth Barrett*
                    Biographies Pages 596

**Gleanings In Genesis (volume I)** by *Arthur W. Pink*     ISBN: *1-59462-130-6*   **$27.45**
*Appropriately has Genesis been termed "the seed plot of the Bible" for in it we have, in germ form, almost all of the great doctrines which are afterwards fully developed in the books of Scripture which follow...*          Religion/Inspirational Pages 420

**The Master Key** by *L. W. de Laurence*     ISBN: *1-59462-001-6*   **$30.95**
*In no branch of human knowledge has there been a more lively increase of the spirit of research during the past few years than in the study of Psychology, Concentration and Mental Discipline. The requests for authentic lessons in Thought Control, Mental Discipline and...*          New Age/Business Pages 422

**The Lesser Key Of Solomon Goetia** by *L. W. de Laurence*     ISBN: *1-59462-092-X*   **$9.95**
*This translation of the first book of the "Lernegton" which is now for the first time made accessible to students of Talismanic Magic was done, after careful collation and edition, from numerous Ancient Manuscripts in Hebrew, Latin, and French...*          New Age/Occult Pages 92

**Rubaiyat Of Omar Khayyam** by *Edward Fitzgerald*     ISBN: *1-59462-332-5*   **$13.95**
*Edward Fitzgerald, whom the world has already learned, in spite of his own efforts to remain within the shadow of anonymity, to look upon as one of the rarest poets of the century, was born at Bredfield, in Suffolk, on the 31st of March, 1809. He was the third son of John Purcell...*          Music Pages 172

**Ancient Law** by *Henry Maine*     ISBN: *1-59462-128-4*   **$29.95**
*The chief object of the following pages is to indicate some of the earliest ideas of mankind, as they are reflected in Ancient Law, and to point out the relation of those ideas to modern thought.*          Religion/History Pages 452

**Far-Away Stories** by *William J. Locke*     ISBN: *1-59462-129-2*   **$19.45**
*"Good wine needs no bush, but a collection of mixed vintages does. And this book is just such a collection. Some of the stories I do not want to remain buried for ever in the museum files of dead magazine-numbers an author's not unpardonable vanity..."*          Fiction Pages 272

**Life of David Crockett** by *David Crockett*     ISBN: *1-59462-250-7*   **$27.45**
*"Colonel David Crockett was one of the most remarkable men of the times in which he lived. Born in humble life, but gifted with a strong will, an indomitable courage, and unremitting perseverance...*          Biographies/New Age Pages 424

**Lip-Reading** by *Edward Nitchie*     ISBN: *1-59462-206-X*   **$25.95**
*Edward B. Nitchie, founder of the New York School for the Hard of Hearing, now the Nitchie School of Lip-Reading, Inc, wrote "LIP-READING Principles and Practice". The development and perfecting of this meritorious work on lip-reading was an undertaking...*          How-to Pages 400

**A Handbook of Suggestive Therapeutics, Applied Hypnotism, Psychic Science**     ISBN: *1-59462-214-0*   **$24.95**
by *Henry Munro*
                    Health/New Age/Health/Self-help Pages 376

**A Doll's House: and Two Other Plays** by *Henrik Ibsen*     ISBN: *1-59462-112-8*   **$19.95**
*Henrik Ibsen created this classic when in revolutionary 1848 Rome. Introducing some striking concepts in playwriting for the realist genre, this play has been studied the world over.*          Fiction/Classics/Plays 308

**The Light of Asia** by *sir Edwin Arnold*     ISBN: *1-59462-204-3*   **$13.95**
*In this poetic masterpiece, Edwin Arnold describes the life and teachings of Buddha. The man who was to become known as Buddha to the world was born as Prince Gautama of India but he rejected the worldly riches and abandoned the reigns of power when...*          Religion/History/Biographies Pages 170

**The Complete Works of Guy de Maupassant** by *Guy de Maupassant*     ISBN: *1-59462-157-8*   **$16.95**
*"For days and days, nights and nights, I had dreamed of that first kiss which was to consecrate our engagement, and I knew not on what spot I should put my lips..."*          Fiction/Classics Pages 240

**The Art of Cross-Examination** by *Francis L. Wellman*     ISBN: *1-59462-309-0*   **$26.95**
*Written by a renowned trial lawyer, Wellman imparts his experience and uses case studies to explain how to use psychology to extract desired information through questioning.*          How-to/Science/Reference Pages 408

**Answered or Unanswered?** by *Louisa Vaughan*     ISBN: *1-59462-248-5*   **$10.95**
*Miracles of Faith in China*
                    Religion Pages 112

**The Edinburgh Lectures on Mental Science (1909)** by *Thomas*     ISBN: *1-59462-008-3*   **$11.95**
*This book contains the substance of a course of lectures recently given by the writer in the Queen Street Hall, Edinburgh. Its purpose is to indicate the Natural Principles governing the relation between Mental Action and Material Conditions...*          New Age/Psychology Pages 148

**Ayesha** by *H. Rider Haggard*     ISBN: *1-59462-301-5*   **$24.95**
*Verily and indeed it is the unexpected that happens! Probably if there was one person upon the earth from whom the Editor of this, and of a certain previous history, did not expect to hear again...*          Classics Pages 380

**Ayala's Angel** by *Anthony Trollope*     ISBN: *1-59462-352-X*   **$29.95**
*The two girls were both pretty, but Lucy who was twenty-one who supposed to be simple and comparatively unattractive, whereas Ayala was credited, as her Bombwhat romantic name might show, with poetic charm and a taste for romance. Ayala when her father died was nineteen...*          Fiction Pages 484

**The American Commonwealth** by *James Bryce*     ISBN: *1-59462-286-8*   **$34.45**
*An interpretation of American democratic political theory. It examines political mechanics and society from the perspective of Scotsman James Bryce*
                    Politics Pages 572

**Stories of the Pilgrims** by *Margaret P. Pumphrey*     ISBN: *1-59462-116-0*   **$17.95**
*This book explores pilgrims religious oppression in England as well as their escape to Holland and eventual crossing to America on the Mayflower, and their early days in New England...*          History Pages 268

QTY

**The Fasting Cure** *by Sinclair Upton*                                    ISBN: *1-59462-222-1*  **$13.95**

*In the Cosmopolitan Magazine for May, 1910, and in the Contemporary Review (London) for April, 1910, I published an article dealing with my experiences in fasting. I have written a great many magazine articles, but never one which attracted so much attention...  New Age/Self Help/Health Pages 164*

**Hebrew Astrology** *by Sepharial*                                        ISBN: *1-59462-308-0*  **$13.45**

*In these days of advanced thinking it is a matter of common observation that we have left many of the old landmarks behind and that we are now pressing forward to greater heights and to a wider horizon than that which represented the mind-content of our progenitors...  Astrology Pages 144*

**Thought Vibration or The Law of Attraction in the Thought World**        ISBN: *1-59462-127-6*  **$12.95**

*by William Walker Atkinson*                                                *Psychology/Religion Pages 144*

**Optimism** *by Helen Keller*                                             ISBN: *1-59462-108-X*  **$15.95**

*Helen Keller was blind, deaf, and mute since 19 months old, yet famously learned how to overcome these handicaps, communicate with the world, and spread her lectures promoting optimism.  An inspiring read for everyone...  Biographies/Inspirational Pages 84*

**Sara Crewe** *by Frances Burnett*                                        ISBN: *1-59462-360-0*  **$9.45**

*In the first place, Miss Minchin lived in London. Her home was a large, dull, tall one, in a large, dull square, where all the houses were alike, and all the sparrows were alike, and where all the door-knockers made the same heavy sound...  Childrens/Classic Pages 88*

**The Autobiography of Benjamin Franklin** *by Benjamin Franklin*          ISBN: *1-59462-135-7*  **$24.95**

*The Autobiography of Benjamin Franklin has probably been more extensively read than any other American historical work, and no other book of its kind has had such ups and downs of fortune. Franklin lived for many years in England, where he was agent...  Biographies/History Pages 332*

| Name | |
|---|---|
| Email | |
| Telephone | |
| Address | |
| | |
| City, State ZIP | |

☐ **Credit Card**          ☐ **Check / Money Order**

| Credit Card Number | |
|---|---|
| Expiration Date | |
| Signature | |

*Please Mail to:   Book Jungle*
*PO Box 2226*
*Champaign, IL 61825*
*or Fax to:      630-214-0564*

## ORDERING INFORMATION

**web**: *www.bookjungle.com*
**email**: *sales@bookjungle.com*
**fax**: *630-214-0564*
**mail**: *Book Jungle  PO Box 2226  Champaign, IL 61825*
**or PayPal** *to sales@bookjungle.com*

*Please contact us for bulk discounts*

## DIRECT-ORDER TERMS

**20% Discount if You Order
Two or More Books**
Free Domestic Shipping!
Accepted: Master Card, Visa,
Discover, American Express

www.ingramcontent.com/pod-product-compliance
Lightning Source LLC
Chambersburg PA
CBHW080824020726

47501CB00009B/2414